UNTHREADED

H.B. Cavalier

nowhere press

First Edition

First printing, March 2022
Revised, March 2024

ISBN 978-1-73408-662-1

Nowhere Press
PO Box 314
Corvallis, OR 97339

nowherepress.com
unthreaded.net

Book design by Ian Cavalier

Twenty percent of the net profits from sales of this book will be donated to the 501(c)(3) charity Refugees International.

For the victims of the *Lancastria* sinking,
and everyone else that time forgot.

CONTENTS

SPOOL

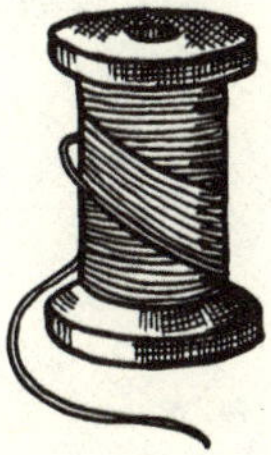

I WAS BORN on July 6, 1906, just in time for breakfast. A strange thing to know, given all I've forgotten, yet know it, I do – with a bright, electric certainty – though I can only guess at my name. There's merely a note, a strum, the faintest of tremors: Avrum, Rudy – something like Reuven. Yes, Reuven. Not sure how that would taste if I had a mouth, but the feeling is right. Just enough tension to snap me back.

It's settled then. My name was Reuven.

Even if it wasn't.

I have nothing to say about my birth; I can't recall the story, and it's far too late to ask. I simply settled into my skin and called it good – letting the world enfold and embrace me, as we all do in the beginning. Giving myself completely to life. To fickle breath and tender mood. To instinct and love and Poland – or what once was and would again be Poland. One of the defining features of my time was the redrawing of the map: again and again, often with violence. I'd come to love drawing myself, but usually managed it without any bloodshed. I was fairly quiet, though. Not one to impose my illustrations on others. I never did take up much space.

My first home was little more than a shack, tucked away in a sleepy, shrinking village not far from Białystok. An easy memory, even for me; there's hardly anything to recall. If my shtetl wasn't already a ghost town, it was surely on its deathbed. I can't unearth its name, of course, yet hesitate to take the blame for that. It's possible it didn't even have a name.

I could be wrong, though. You forget a lot of things when you blow your own brains out.

But I'm getting ahead of myself.

Either way, my village had an irreparable leak. Pogroms and depression had driven out many, and the remainder steadily drained as I learned to walk and talk. I always knew my family would follow when we had the chance. Few things tied us to that place, and only one really mattered: my grandfather. A widely respected rabbi in his day, my mother was his youngest child and his dedicated caretaker. I remember him in strong streaks of black and white: a hunched shadow with an ashen face, pale beard giving him the look of something slowly melting. Which he was, in a way, though more on the inside than out. While he could recite Tehillim like he was reading, he rarely recognized the people around him – including my mother. A real pity, given all she did for him.

And for me.

Despite her impish, erratic impulses, my mother was a natural nurse. Or maybe the nursing itself fueled her absurdity. Perhaps it was the sleep I stole that forged her dark humor, my own infirmity driving her eccentricities. Perhaps I robbed her of her sanity.

There's a thought.

But again, I'm losing the plot. Forgive me. We don't have much time here, and I know you have things to do. I won't ask you to sacrifice as my mother did. I'm not sure how healthy it was for her.

Of all her sacrifices, she seemed least happy staying in that cold, muddy village while my father went west without us. I'm not sure how many times this happened, or for how long, or why, or who enabled it. I'm not sure of much at all – but I know I didn't mind. I chased geese and dug potatoes, and did what I could to lift my mother's moods. But those moods were hers alone.

Her name was Rivka, I believe, and she was a beauty. With thick dark hair, a small mouth, and large, wide-set eyes, her delicate looks belied a wild spirit. She laughed easily, loved the outdoors, and had a peculiar, rather masculine mind. As much as I wished, she never did coddle me. She respected me too much for that. I was more than her son, even as a child. I was her accomplice, her "little bird" with the whistling lungs, her comedic match. I was her friend.

My father's name is lost to me. A stocky man with a chestnut beard, memories of him are a bit harder to siphon from this gloom. What does stand out, though – what glows in the dark, if you will – is the way he looked at me. All those quizzical faces. That man never did know what to make of me. We shared a mutual appreciation, but there wasn't much overlap between us. Not much connection. He was all business at heart, spending my youth undoing his farming roots and learning a "respectable trade." So westward he'd go, following his brothers into the diamond industry.

His business ventures were prompted by me, at least in part. By the time his trips began – whatever they entailed – I'd cut something of a hole in the family purse. My first few winters had taken a toll, leaving me weak, difficult, and expensive. I didn't have many asthma attacks in the village, but enough to require house calls and medicines – none of which were free. More costly still were trips to Białystok (which I found breathtaking, if you'll excuse the pun), where doctors would poke and prod and charm me with their myriad metal devices. And these luxuries were hardly optional: I was a creature of extremes, even then. My attacks, rare though they were, invariably brought me near the point of death.

I didn't fully understand the danger then. I saw each flare-up as a bizarre (if terrifying) exception to normalcy that, once behind me, wouldn't possibly think to strike again. Time only marched forward, after all. Episodes came and went like fleeting nightmares; afterward I would wake and forget. I was still free then, only at the entrance of that mirrored maze of panic and paranoia. I could still see the world around me. Could still breathe the fresh, country air. How could any illness stretch into perpetuity? In the amnesic fog of childhood, I couldn't fathom perpetuity of *any* kind, at all.

And yet, here we are.

But back to then.

My sister Adah was born on November 8, 1910, when my father was away. I tell you, I marvel at my recollection of these dates. I've lost my favorite songs and books, and all that's left of my surname is the letter B. Why birthdays didn't follow suit is beyond me. The bullet must've missed them.

Life felt cramped with a new baby. Our hovel hadn't the space for more people, but this issue soon resolved itself; my grandfather died mere weeks after Adah's birth. Not that he really *lived* those last years. Physically, he remained, but on most other fronts he'd already passed. Until the end, he'd walk me through our gutted village, to the tiny cheder in which I learned to read and write – but he didn't know whose hand he held. Habit alone told his feet where to go.

With so few people, it's a wonder we had a school at all. Goods mostly came from a neighboring town, as did the news. Gossip and music, flavor and fun, all that brought color to our lives lay kilometers away – in a *real* shtetl. And though I couldn't call it home, its pounding heart would beat within me, on some level, for the rest of my life. However far I strayed from my roots, however anglicized I became, however "abstruse" (as my father claimed), I always held a kernel of that world within me. My hands would never stop touching what I'd touched there.

What is existence, after all, but a collection of events? An unending mosaic, kaleidoscopic and shifting. A baffling web of ancestry and forgotten lives, spun by the secret aims of our souls.

But what was I saying?

Oh yes, the cheder.

My early education was woefully austere: half a dozen boys in a one-room hut, squinting at holy books under dim lamps. But my path was bright nonetheless, illuminated by the influence of Mussar – a philosophy that followed my family as surely as cholent and challah. While my maternal line bore mystical hearts, my father's stuck to the head, spurring rigorous study and relentless, inward-facing scrutiny. No corner of my soul escaped the light, every aspect of my character polished and purified for the highest good (or so my parents hoped). Throughout my life, our house remained a playground of moral mind games, difficult scenarios laid out like obstacle courses. Politics, disagreements, my sister's taste in clothes: all passed through a *Mussar filter* with which we'd refine our objectives while taming our baser natures.

In that laboratory, I became a scientist. An ethics calculator. A spiritual alchemist. And I always felt grateful for this, especially after knowing those raised without such a system. What an immense headache, concocting one from scratch!

Of course, ready-made philosophies do have their shortcomings. Rather serious ones, in some cases.

But I'll get to that.

BOBBIN

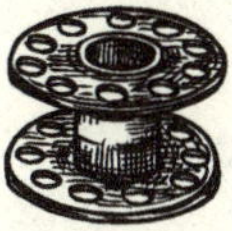

IT PROBABLY GOES without saying that my death was a bit jarring. A monumental jolt, in fact – a gargantuan response to one claustrophobic second. Swift and harsh and absolute. But only fleeting. A fairly typical triumph for me: thorough but brief.

Nothing lasts forever, after all. Not even nothing.

Awash as I am in this ink and tar, it can be hard to see the past swimming by – but even in the beginning, when the black was at its thickest, I had no trouble recognizing Belgium. I could feel myself running, skinny and coal-smeared, behind a flock of boys – Jewish boys like me – down an artery of tracks in the clatter of Antwerp. I can't tell you how I got there. Beyond a lengthy stay in Poznań, I have no memory of the trip. But I do know I was happy to call it home.

Yet I didn't miss it much when we fled, chased off by fire and bombs just a year later. I was seven when we arrived and eight when we left – hardly enough time to suffer true loss. It was only after the war, when friends and family returned and we didn't, that I began to feel displaced.

But we're not there yet. Do forgive my rambling. Making sense of these scraps is hard enough; organizing them is almost beyond me. But I need to, and soon. I don't know how much time I have. This place feels like a closing book. It was much more spacious before – though without these walls, I'd have no memories at all. It's only under pressure that anything becomes solid.

All the same, I'll get on with my story.

My father took a merchant role in his brothers' business, which – now that I think about it – was likely what he'd been doing all along. I can never be sure, though. As I said, I wasn't too close with him. Both of my uncles cut diamonds, and I'd visit them at work from time to time. It was my introversion that allowed for this: my decidedly un-childlike ability to hold still and stay silent – though these were among the very traits my father found so eccentric. Our views were at odds, more often than not; he simply didn't feel what I felt. He took no notice of the texture of his clothes, seemed immune to the tension of crowds, and was baffled by the mere *thought* of noise having flavor (though my mother took delight in discussing which sounds tasted best).

On rare occasion, my father would take me to a gem dealer or a jewelry store, testing the waters for someday teaching me the trade. I'd listen to him haggle and watch him sign papers, but I was far more interested in the finished products – glistening bracelets on artificial wrists, gaudy necklaces in glass boxes – than the banalities of buying and selling.

The man tried, though, he really did. And it'd be a lie to say we had nothing in common. Time would give us plenty to agree on: books, chess, unnecessarily complicated debates. What's more, he was always gentle with me. Stable and protective. My health demanded a heedful vigilance that he cordially abided by. Unfortunately, his study of me went far beyond allergies and weather patterns. Dissecting my habits and proclivities, he likely found plenty he didn't like. I'm sure he uncovered my secrets long before I did.

He wouldn't have been the only one. I was always the last to know.

I went to a much bigger school in Antwerp, and a much bigger synagogue. The sheer volume of people even granted me a few friends. The city offered a variety of doctors, as well, and my lungs were privy to cutting-edge experimentation. Little came of it, however; in the umbral quilt of our narrow house, we compiled a short list of what helped, and a terribly long one of what didn't. Coffee, by far, was my preferred remedy. Burnt, bitter earth in a cup: more delicious than any tonic I was forced to choke down, and probably just as effective. My mother was always happy to brew it, no matter the hour – stealing sips while teasing me about my zest for "the nightlife."

I can almost taste it now.

Perhaps you can, too.

Overflows are common, I'm afraid. There's simply nothing to hold me together now, without skin. I do tend to dissipate. Dissolved in the past, devoured by memories: short pants and flat caps, curls cropped, nose running, awash in the patchwork peelings of ornate buildings. Colors disjointed and fractalized, swimming like eels, woven with smoke and fish, the cry of newsboys, the clop of hooves, the unyielding threat of women's hats. Oh, those hats! Monstrous things. Like cakes, like hawks' nests, deformed and excessive, stealing eyes in their diabolical shadows.

It's no wonder I got into fashion. The needle was my sword; I was born for a holy war.

But this has to stop! I can't start dreaming now. I need to stay awake!

Which brings me back to coffee.

Surely, you drink coffee. Would you have a little now? For me? To help me remember? Just one favor, I promise I won't ask for more. My mother brewed it dark. Very dark.

Oh, my mother.

She thrived in Antwerp, making friends fast, never shying from a long chat. And not only Yiddish, but Dutch, German, and even the lullaby language of Hebrew were at her disposal – to say nothing of Polish. Somehow, I hadn't realized how worldly she was. Or how social. At shul, her side of the mechitza was like a clucking henhouse. I never knew what they were talking about, though. I'd be with my father, and usually at a loss for words.

I wonder, sometimes, how life might've unfolded in Belgium: bonding with my uncles, learning to shape a diamond, enjoying a familial intimacy that may or may not have become oppressive. Would things have been different there, or was I born for what I was born for, unalterably? Could Antwerp really have diffused the ticking time bomb within me, foiling an explosion of obliterating love? Does anything have such power? To unstitch the universe? Or are we all bound, irrevocably, to plans that we made ourselves?

You'd think I'd know these things by now.

Fate or no fate, if I had to guess, I'd say moving to England was for the best. Mine was a London-sized heart, after all, trapped in a shtetl boy's chest.

It's no wonder I couldn't breathe.

EYE

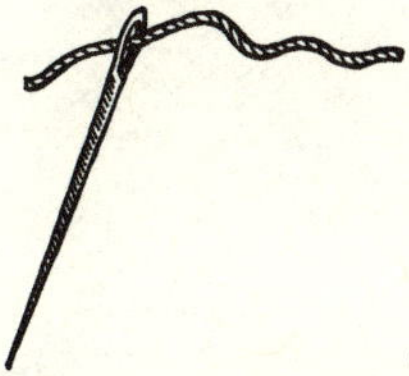

I TURNED EIGHT in 1914. The Death Year.

First, it was the neighbor boy. Eli, if I recall. Charismatic, popular, and right around my age, he fell from a roof throwing rocks at a train – taking the whole community down with him. In gutted silence, we brought his family food, and as my mother cleaned their dishes I witnessed the full, naked brutality of grief. This wasn't mere mourning, no: this was death come twice. That child's parents weren't weeping: they *screamed.* Stabbed clean through with weapons I could almost see. Collapsed and groping, but unable to remove the blades.

None of it was for my eyes. I shouldn't have been there. Yet on and on I watched, frozen on an icy island of numbing dread. Few feelings bloomed in those desolate wastes, but guilt could. And it did. Pale, strange, and withdrawn as I was, I was barely a shadow of that dead boy – yet still alive. And for what?

Right then and there, I made an oath: to make my life count. To withstand my body's onslaughts and make something of myself. Spare my loved ones this ungodly anguish. I would never fall, I told my mother.

I was her "little bird," after all. I could fly. I would fight and I would win and I would *live*.

I *promised*.

Oh, me. I told you I was a creature of extremes.

I was far from alone in that, though. All of Europe seemed to be simmering in feverish, confused conviction. Our city felt crowded somehow. Anxious. Stuffed with evacuees from some unseen disaster. We liked to think it was a safe place, and carried on with our daily tasks, ignoring the news and the whine of intuition – giving the sky the benefit of the doubt until the very moment it fell.

We learned nothing from this, mind you. Decades later, we'd replay this passivity on an even grander stage. But that's human nature, I suppose. Morbid and myopic. So richly imaginative, it would sooner weave a tapestry of excuses than heed common sense. It's almost like people *want* to get bombed. In which case, what can I say? You can't learn without a lesson. And besides, it's not my world anymore. My judgments are moot. No one ever listens to the dead.

Where was I?

Oh yes: the bombs. Antwerp, on fire in the middle of the night.

My father was away on business, as he often was. Paris, perhaps? I'm not sure. I was young and, well, you know – this head wound hasn't done me any favors. I can't offer details. I can only guarantee the strength of my feelings. That's all you keep, in the end: the branding on your soul. Aching or ecstatic, loved or loathed, whatever you can't set down or wash off or squirm your way out of, that's what you get. That's what you are.

So forgive me for lacking in facts and figures. I'm not the world's most reliable narrator. In fact, I've even forgotten how this conversation began. God knows why I'm telling this story; all I know is that I *must*.

My mother woke Adah and me in the dark, and without our father we ran. Without books, without photos, without letters or heirlooms. Without medicine for anything, body or soul. And Antwerp ran with us. Through smoke and flame, confusion and pain, under the low, ghostly trumpets of judgment day. Ignoring Adah's complaints, ignoring my lungs, ignoring all but the creaking, fire-belching sky. Only with the zeppelins safely behind us – those groaning, night-cloaked death hippos – did we slow.

Dawn broke over a city of animated corpses, mindless and drained in the blue light, instinctively migrating to the sea. Strangers of all stripes, we were: a classless alliance of silent shock. When I collapsed, a man lifted me, for my mother's arms were full with Adah. I'd never seen that man before, and would never see him after. My mother said nothing but "thank you." He said nothing at all.

History recorded what happened next – the mass exodus, clogging docks for days, if not weeks, boats crammed to overflowing – but I myself hardly bore witness. We were among the lucky ones, ushered aboard a repurposed fishing vessel mere hours after our arrival. My obvious suffering earned our passage;

apparently I put on quite the show. It was neither the first nor the last asthmatic miracle I'd perform in my life, but it did go down as the most celebrated. My family was whisked ahead of the crowds and sent on our way with haste.

Even then, even there, the kindness of strangers didn't waver. It was a force I'd come to depend on in life. Humans really are mostly good, believe it or not. They just need the chance to prove it.

Crushed both by asthma and a mob of refugees, I spent that trip stranded somewhere I'd rather not revisit. Yet, that's exactly what I'm given to recall. Not the name of my father nor my hometown. Not my favorite restaurants, where I'd gaze over countless meals into the smiling eyes of my lover, sated by a honeyed bliss.

No, no. None of that.

What I remember instead is my mother, hoisting me up and hauling me to the deck rail, propping me in the pummeling wind so I might get some air.

And I remember a child, no more than two, squirming in a woman's arms nearby. Round cheeks, white bonnet, huge blue eyes. I remember her twisting about. I remember her lurching. And I remember her dropping smooth and straight over the edge of the boat.

Slip.

Gone.

Once paired, some things just never part: a smell and a place, a song and a mood, a drink and one hell of a hangover. Suffice it to say, my asthma was not improved by the vision of an infant's death.

The damage was done, though.

The woman, of course, started screaming. A seismic tremor. A mutant, wailing cacophony. One man restrained her, pulling her back from the edge. Another offered to jump in himself. But everyone knew it was too late. The ship sailed on.

Slip.

Gone.

Etched deeper with every smothering attack, that memory is part of me now – a creeping phantom sure to follow me into my next life, masked as some mysterious phobia one hundred years from now.

Slip.

Gone.

That is what I remember. Not the title I held at my company. Not my favorite prayers or passages. Not even my own bar mitzvah.

That.

NEEDLE

WE LANDED IN England, and were welcomed with English manners: put in an inn, given papers and permissions, allowed to wait out the nightmare we'd managed to escape. The process was rocky, though. We had no money, couldn't speak the language, weren't Belgian citizens, and posed a bureaucratic imbroglio in my father's absence. But my father arrived soon enough, pulled a few strings, and settled us into a dreadful little flat in London's East End – where I promptly became a veritable invalid.

Time explained things, as it often does: that it was smoke and dander, mold and soot causing my suffering. But all I knew at the time was I was surely going to die. Overnight I went from a playful child to a prisoner of war, held captive and tortured by my own lungs, with no clue what information they were trying to wrench from me. Two, three, even four times a week, my tormentors entered my chamber, assailing me for hours on end, without explanation – leaving me purple in my pleas for mercy, even knocking me unconscious. I was winded at my best, exhausted to my soul, aching in ways I never knew possible. And God help me should I ever catch a cold.

My captors weren't invincible, though, and as the years marched on, my arsenal of treatments grew. With nebulizers, vaporizers, and medicated cigarettes, I'd force the enemy to retreat. Time gave me diets and therapy, suburbs and the sea, and the healing devilry of love. But during the Great War, time was no friend to me. Waiting for the doctor and his wizardly injections, time was only an accomplice, sadistic in its apathy as it devoured my childhood.

To neighboring kids, I was phantasmal. Monstrous. An experiment, perhaps, a reanimated corpse. So rarely seen, I was hardly more than myth. And it fell on Adah to defend me, sparking a mutual jealousy that singed even our happiest days. My sister had health and freedom and indisputable intelligence – but I got all the attention. She wasn't above jumping on my bed while I refilled my inhaler.

I was cursed and I knew it. So I did the only thing I could do: I became an optimist.

Every burden hides a blessing, after all – even then, I knew that. My capacity for gratitude ballooned: a full, easy breath delivered a euphoric rainbow of flavors, and my very survival seemed no less than divine providence. From death itself God plucked me, quite literally – but not before showing me the full scope of His love. When the cold night came that I finally succumbed, my end brought visions of sanctity so beautiful I was almost disappointed to recover. Cradled in light, cleansed and free, I rapturously absorbed the one message – the fundamental, unambiguous truth – that would guide me for the rest of my life: *nothing done in love can ever be wrong.*

My first death didn't last long, of course; mere minutes in the realm of the living. The keening of my parents called me back – along with a whopping dose of adrenaline. I didn't resist. To comfort the grieving, to bring down death's ecstasy for all to know – that would be my mission.

Or so I hoped.

I shared my experience as soon as I could, preaching to anyone who would listen. But my revelations were dreamy and vague, and people tired of them in time. Ultimately, death only set me further apart. I kept it close, though. Holy and precious, it clouded my eyes, making everything sacred. Food and drink, the cinnamon song of birds, the sun on my face: divine kisses, all of it. And I, myself: a miracle. An uncertain, nerve-racking miracle.

As you can imagine, none of this helped my social life. I missed a tremendous amount of schooling, socializing, and – shall we say – *normalizing* in my confinement. I taught myself to draw and sew, managed piano lessons alright, and developed the sagely intellect of a rabbi – but I had no friends and little knowledge of my surroundings. I learned English in a void, lacking all sense of pronunciation or flow; Adah had practically mastered phonetics before I could even converse. I had fallen behind, and never did catch up. Shell-shocked by my body, I tiptoed through life, suspicious and jumpy, ever braced for attack. Mystically sensitive, profoundly observant, and not relatable in the slightest.

My memories of the East End come only in flashes: tight streets, rancid smells, laundry unlikely to ever dry. Angry, aggressive children I avoided like allergens. Nostalgia would say there was community, a messy camaraderie, a current of inspiration woven through the crime and violence and need: interesting events, radical ideas, charming characters. But it was filthy! The alleys were like chimneys, inhospitable channels of soot. Poverty was ubiquitous and no one ever seemed to be in a good mood.

What a strange illusionist memory is: daring to claim that the more you suffer, the more you truly live. The more *real* you are, the more *vibrant*, *creative*, *wise.* Honoring resilience is fair, but holding lack as a virtue? I can only hope in my next life I have the wits not to glamorize misery, not to sanctify some mythic pornography of woundedness – at least not for too terribly long. God forbid I *identify* with it. That's the last thing I need after what I've done.

But we'll see. It's a very human thing to do.

For now, at least, I know where I stand: the East End tried to *kill* me, so I'm not too sentimental about it. Faith alone bore me through those years. Faith, and the idiot compulsions of habit. Death may have tempered my bitterness, but you'll never catch the dead being maudlin.

Still, it could've been worse. I developed a case of gallows humor, after all, not psychosis. I have my mother to thank for that. It's clear now that my episodes terrified her, that in private she prepared for my funeral – but at the time she never showed it. She showed nothing but confidence, in fact: in goodness, in God, in my own dubious will. Yet she never left my side. Even with a day job doing laundry, she gave her nights to me – mending clothes, mixing medicines, singing all the while. From sheer boredom, she'd soothe me in Hebrew, though I barely understood it beyond prayer – endearing me to its music far more than its meaning. I knew by now she was an intellectual, a highly literate woman from an educated family, with several siblings in positions of spiritual leadership – so watching her talk to sock puppets, laugh at her own jokes, and spin in circles to stay awake was heartbreaking. She was wasted on me. But not once did I hear her complain. "What else would I be doing at this hour, Ruvi? All the shops are closed!"

Meanwhile, my father busied himself with business, ultimately winning friends in Hatton Garden and putting down roots. I've no idea how he evaded deportation. "Russians" like us were hardly a welcome class, to say nothing of Jews. But these struggles were hidden from me; it was clear I had enough stress. Whatever spells were cast worked, though. At the end of the war, most of our kin returned to Belgium (with a few opting for Holland), while my father had established himself as a reliable diamond dealer. His reputation alone might've earned him British citizenship, but it was probably his pocketbook that sealed the deal – just as it gave me a new lease on life.

In 1918, we bought a house in Stamford Hill: a two-story end-terrace bordering an empty, grassy lot. And none too soon. The flu was fast approaching the crowded East End, and surely would've finished me off. Instead, I was cautiously quarantined through the worst of it in an airy, fresh new home. Crisp and green all around, it could've been the countryside compared to where I'd been, yet we suffered no lack of amenities; a well-stocked kosher grocer kept shop just blocks away, and I was *ravenous*. For the first time since coming to London, I could eat. Not just nibble, not just get by. No: I was a human vacuum, guzzling my surroundings indiscriminately, all but chewing the furniture for the sheer pleasure – for at last, I could *breathe*. I must've grown six inches that year.

Bodies are curious things, aren't they? What strange plumbing. Like some self-consuming tongue, life rises from the earth only to fold over and slurp at its own origins. It's scarcely more than cannibalism.

I can't say I love having a body – especially the human variety. A poorly fitted one can be downright torturous, but a well-tailored form is hardly any better. I find them all rather unwieldy, to be honest. Itchy and achy at the best of times. Once you wear one, though, you do tend to get stuck. After so much contorting just to fit, you need all kinds of adjustments – and it takes a whole new body to correct for the old! It becomes an addiction, drawing you back with increasing frequency. First, an Anatolian midwife, then a scribe in China. A shepherd on the Aegean. An Israelite bride. In Rome, a priestess; in Gaul, a druid; in Tibet, a monk. And in the wilds of Italy: a starry-eyed follower of Saint Francis. I knew bliss as an

Iñupiaq mother, and grief in the Inquisition, watching my lover burn. I knew the Andes as a nun, and Arabia as the untamed daughter of a Muslim botanist. Faster and faster, these lives pile up – devout and hungry, grasping homesick for the heavens yet slipping ever further away. The next thing you know, you're up to your neck. You wake up one morning, a powerful Brahmin in India, and see with gruesome clarity the pain you've caused aiding British imperialism. And then you know it's got you. There's no way out now.

Naturally, next would come the asthmatic immigrant. Having used my voice against my people, it only made sense give it up. To cut short my words with breathlessness, to suffer coughing fits and laryngitis, a whole mesh of muting comorbidities. And of course, to carry all the while a most adamantine accent.

It's a pity my psychic noose didn't make me more effective at helping others. It hardly whittled down my pride, either; I never did cope well with embarrassment. Perhaps my efforts were misguided.

I tried, at least. I'll figure it out eventually.

But I'm afraid I'm rambling again. These memories do meander, always spilling such compelling inkblots. Makes me feel a little drunk at times. Do forgive me.

Back to my story.

The years have folded Stamford Hill into London's entrails, but at the end of the Great War it felt like a retreat. The air was lighter, the rooms bigger, the future brighter. Yet my sun didn't fully rise until the summer of 1919, for it was then that I was at last released into the wild. My lungs had built some strength, and I showed a maturity and piousness that most parents only dream of. So I was set loose: to follow my impulses, to chase my dreams. To lie in the park all day, eating nothing but pickles, scones, and ice cream. But my first act – my first genuine move as a sturdy, self-determined young man – was to attend the Victory Parade.

Oh, the Victory Parade! There's no describing the relief bubbling through the city that day. A relief like glee, a relief I knew intimately. And the soldiers, marching like sardines through the streets: they mirrored my state, as well. Their battles had also passed. They, too, had emerged victorious. Never mind that their success was met with cheers, and mine with trepidation. Never mind that their uniforms, smacking of pride and bravery, clashed with my somber garb. I didn't feel insecure. Alone in a crowd, I wasn't the least bit anxious.

I was absolutely mesmerized.

These were heroes filing by: Tommies in tight formation, some scarcely able to repress their grins. Ruddy-cheeked, strong-jawed, suggestively roguish. Armed with rifles and flags and enviable decorum. Icons, now. Idols. Something to emulate. Something to study. Something to . . . *something.*

I won't pretend that I knew what I was feeling then, however obvious it is now. At the time, though, I hadn't a clue. All I knew was that I was liked what I saw. Maybe a little too much.

I was thirteen.

FOLD

ADAH WAS THIRTEEN when she cut her hair, dropped the "h" from her name, and acquired a most peculiar dress. That age hit her just as hard as it hit me, and though the reasons were comparably benign, the effect was much more dramatic. Unwilling to open my own Pandora's box, I appreciated Adah's – or should I say *Ada's* – pioneering spirit. So when my father railed against her skirt length, and my mother grieved like there'd been a death, I took my sister's side. We didn't live in a shtetl anymore. We lived in *London*. She was only trying to fit in.

Not that I did.

My English still lagged, and I had little to say, anyway. I felt like a balloon, blown between the ecstasies of faith and the ache of isolation. A fragile bird on a high wind. Numinous dreams, brushes with death, and a helpless, holy trust had stirred in me a need to serve, to seek, to make sense of my continued existence. But I felt alone in my mystical musings, even at shul. Ours was the god of intellect, the god of civilization – but the life I led wasn't theoretical. Reason and philosophy held no power without air.

The inhalation and exhalation of soul, that curiously physical link to the divine: that was my religion. My sublime meditation. My ceaseless prayer. This celestial point of contact – the delicate intersection of eternity and life, forever on my mind – had freed me from temporal abstractions.

I was nothing but heart.

Healing, sacred love, that's what called me: to care, to share. To *merge.* I could feel it, see its glow in every hallowed letter. I could taste it in the maple cream of a soprano, the vanilla of a violin, the daphne and almond of Liszt. "Un Sospiro" left me swooning, enraptured by my own protean senses, more certain than ever of the genius of God. But I couldn't articulate this, and no one seemed to relate. I was stuck on a cloud. I'd come of age with no rhythm, no patterns, not even the steady beat of breath. Nebulous and impractical, I was out of step with those I knew.

And I was no better with strangers. I was certainly no Englishman.

I didn't know what I was.

Zionism spoke to my uprootedness, and studying Hebrew grounded me some, but it was Kabbalah that offered a home. Chasidus, mysticism, the teachings of my mother's family – the tree from which I'd fallen still thrived in a distant, dreamlike land I was constantly reminded (not always kindly) that I belonged. And I ached for it. I pored over books and lingered with elders – in no small part to avoid my peers. The other boys unnerved me somehow, and I feared they'd catch my glances. Feared I'd misspeak. I'd go weeks without wheezing, yet my habits remained solitary: reading, walking, playing piano. Long, lazy hours were given to sketchbooks, where my shyness could make itself useful. With no one to distract me, my illustrations improved rapidly – and it was evident.

Ada recruited my skills just as soon as she noticed them. Before I knew it, my room was filled with women's magazines, fashion plates, sewing patterns. Where Ada got these things was beyond me, but once they entered our home they were as much mine as hers. And so began my fashion career: drawing modified dress concepts to test against our mother.

Our parents were soft people, though, all things considered. Pliable. They listened to their children, in times of peace and otherwise, and Ada was particularly skilled in debates. Even at that age, her intellect was unparalleled – with woefully few outlets. It must have felt excruciating for her, though at the time her bitterness only vexed me. Had our genders been reversed (as perhaps they should've been) she would've made a cunning lawyer. Together, we broke our parents of the need to guide us, and exploited their instinct to simply enjoy us. Unique expressions of God, we were: rare products of a rare time. Repairing the world with modern techniques.

Our arguments were convincing. So convincing, in fact, that I was allowed to anglicize my own name. *Reuben* didn't last long, though. He always sort of felt like a liar.

Our parents were more open to altering clothes than to buying them – or borrowing from Ada's shiksa friends, which she'd amassed in quantity – and I soon realized my knack for tailoring. Ada and I would spend hours on the floor beside the sewing machine, lost in an olio of sketches, threads, and fabric clippings. We were precise in our plans, executing our visions with caution. The resources allotted to us were scanty; mismeasuring was an unforgivable sin.

I remember those days fondly. Having spent my life receiving help, it felt good to offer some in return. Ada became both my protégé and my equal, not only because we discovered this craft side by side, but because she was unquestionably my intellectual match. I'd be caught by surprise talking to her, struck by the sense that I didn't even know her. In all our time together, I'd merely been languishing, absorbed by the needs of my body, hardly a brother at all. For a few years I'd even loathed Ada, dreading her youthful zest when I could scarcely move. Beyond the fits and messes and comical demands of her childhood, I was oblivious to what she'd been up to. But whatever it was, it formed the foundation of one of the saddest, strongest, most brilliant women I would ever know. With the discernment of our father and the linguistic gifts of our mother, she awed me almost daily. The love I felt growing for her was quite fierce indeed.

Oh, that heart of mine.

To feel at such a scale comes naturally *here* – but to stuff it into form, filter it through a human lens? What a terrifying weakness. I certainly didn't manage it well. Ultimately, I would fail Ada, criticizing and condemning her, precisely *because* I cared. Life can blind us to such hypocrisy, but the vision clears soon enough. Death keeps no secrets.

For the time, though, my sister and I were close. Hand in hand on a tightrope, teetering between ancestral ghosts and the future. While Ada's apparel (and my own, increasingly) wasn't quite halachic, there was nothing amoral in our behavior: we were studious children, and Ada was particularly serious. Sullen, even. Her goal was camouflage, not grandstanding, so our parents adjusted in time. Our funds remained tight, though. Meager allowances, a little money Ada made on the side. But what perfect preparation for what I'd go on to do! The rigor required, the efficiency, the exquisite *exactness* demanded in order to waste nothing! I'd later be lauded as "magic" in my precision, but my skills were far from supernatural. They were the results of engrossed obsession, the likes of which only adolescents command.

They were the results of a teenaged boy unable to sow his oats.

Before long, my mother was making use of me, as well – though the alterations I made for her were far less interesting. She'd give Ada and me space when we were together (naturally anxious of provoking her daughter), but when I worked alone she had no shortage of suggestions. I rejected them all. My mother was a keen woman, a genius at wordplay, and a comedic maverick – melting languages together into an uproarious, nonsensical jargon of poetic profanity that regularly had me in hysterics. But she had terrible taste in fashion.

My father was often away. He traveled for work, and not just to Hatton Garden for the day – but to Antwerp, Amsterdam, even Paris. I may have gone with him once or twice, but I've only a hunch. A memory unhinged, lost with the spattered chunks of my skull. I'd assail you with visions of Montmartre in the '20s if I could, but I'm afraid you'll have to settle for lace collars and handkerchief hemlines.

My health was my father's main excuse for not training me, but we both knew there were other reasons. I simply couldn't be trusted around diamonds – at least not in mixed company. I paid attention to all the wrong things, far more taken by glamour and grace than commerce and trade. I should've liked to wear the diamonds myself, in fact – stars on my ears, paired with pearls round my neck – and it was my fatal error to say so aloud. Sewing with my sister, such banter was common. Welcome, even: a sign of insight into the peculiar palate of the urban female. But it wasn't so appreciated around orthodox businessmen. Coupled with my comments on the taste of traffic's growl, I was almost too embarrassing to take out.

So my future remained uncertain.

Rabbinic studies were considered; theology was a passion of mine, after all, and my mother's family had a long tradition of spiritual leadership. But her siblings were ghosts to me, having left the old village years before my birth. Warsaw, Kraków, Katowice,

Łódź – they haunted cities I'd never seen, too far away to light a path for me.

And that's if I could follow in their steps at all.

I certainly had my doubts.

Godly though I was, I couldn't help but worry that long hours in a yeshiva, surrounded by intelligent, interesting young men, might make it hard to focus on Talmudic law. But of course, I couldn't explain that to my parents. I could hardly explain it to myself.

I'm sure you know what I'm getting at, but I can't overstate my ignorance at the time. My fantasies seemed strange, yes, but not *violent* – nothing like the crimes of Sodom and Gomorrah. And I'd yet to be divinely punished for my musings. Still, they were concerning. I found myself thinking about my thoughts almost as often as I thought the thoughts to begin with. Once I even skipped the mikveh before Yom Kippur, feigning sickness to avoid stripping (however piously) near other men, and stayed home to ask God for some clarity.

Neither of us came up with answers.

STITCH

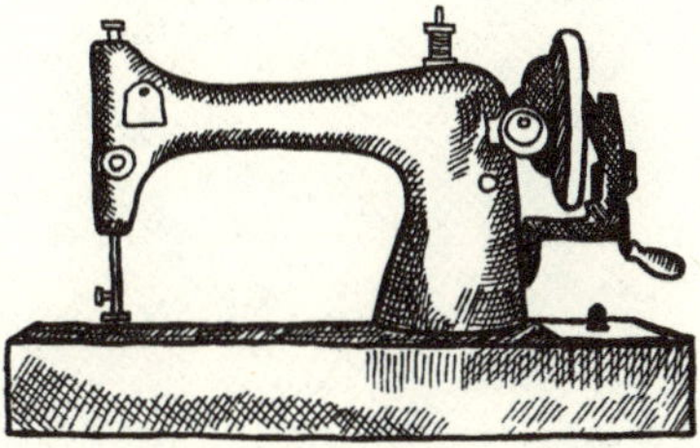

IN THE SPRING of 1925, a colleague of my father paid our home a visit. I can't remember his name, to no surprise, but I do recall he was tall, older than my parents, with a clean-shaven face and sunken cheeks. After my mother let him in, I was the first thing he saw.

I was fairly hard to miss.

I'd been hit with a savage asthma attack the night before. My muscles ached, my chest hurt, and I'm sure I looked a wreck – but I'd spent the whole day napping and was extremely bored with my bed. So I lolled in the front room, pajama-clad and pallid, chatting with my mother as I drew summer dresses.

My father was running late, so the man took a seat near me to wait. Politely, he asked to see what I was sketching. I showed him.

And that was the single most pivotal moment of my life.

Most memories aren't half as vivid. I can conjure up the stew on the stove, onion in the air, steam on the windowpane. My mother at the counter, scarf round her head like the Milky Way. Humming. Piano by the kitchen door, chairs by the fireplace, a medley of lamps and end tables – and me, on the sofa by the stairwell. The base of the ceiling was rimmed with designs: birds and flowers my mother painted, patterns reminiscent of Poland. And above that, three small bedrooms and a bathroom at the top of the stairs. My rumpled bed lay empty, my window closed to the trees. Nightstand littered with remedies: coffee and water. Some sort of tincture. A bottle of ephedrine. A cumbersome atomizer I'd affectionately dubbed "the black balloon."

I was no longer up there, though. No longer under the quilt my aunt had sent from Antwerp, the one my grandmother made decades before. I was lounging downstairs, propped with pillows, sock-feet pointed toward my mother. Itchy-eyed and runny-nosed beside a sad, wrinkled handkerchief. Clipboard in hand, with three sheets of paper. Fingers thin and delicate and pale.

I'm not just rambling now, believe it or not. I set out to tell you what I remember, and this is part of it. It frustrates me as much as you that these recollections aren't more balanced, more democratic – or at least more exciting. What I wouldn't give to bring it all back! Make it whole and real. In truth, sometimes I fear I've made it up. But then back it comes, in violent waves: the *feeling*. The heat of my lover's breath. The rapture, pressing against that body. Sea air through the open window. So vivid, so visceral – there's no room for doubt with memories like that.

But the bouts of blackness are long and heavy, so let me remember this: this random, dreary, unremarkable afternoon, carved into me like a diamond, cut as deep as a sunken babe.

Slip.

Gone.

The page turned. My childhood ended. Adulthood began. In some secret, oracular place, I knew the importance of that moment. My soul saw it – just as that man saw something in my sketches I'd missed.

Unlike most visitors, he was neither from the synagogue nor Hatton Garden. He worked in the clothing industry, as luck would have it, and was consulting with my father about jewelry for a department store fashion show.

At his request, I gave him a whole stack of my drawings.

And there my memory begins to falter.

I can't recall who he connected me with, or how, but things moved fast. Next I know, beyond this murk, is some kind of fashion house. Nothing too fancy, hardly haute couture, but thriving, no less, in the heart of Mayfair – making made-to-order dresses and patterns for stores all over London. Loosed into the whirl of production, I drifted through a warehouse sea of sewing machines, a backroom bog of fabric reels, the swamp of a neighboring tailor's shop, and my own quiet pool: an open office of drafting tables below a row of tall windows, where I was tasked with drawing the package covers of sewing patterns.

That building and the people within it would become my home. Displaced as I'd felt, my work became my culture, my community, my country. And though it was never the objective, my loyalty was handsomely rewarded. My role as a sketcher was only the beginning. I'd ascend the ranks over time, allowing my parents to finally breathe easy – even if I couldn't. No promotion could lift the West End smog or the dust of trimmed fabric, yet I made up for sick days with zeal, winning over my employer with an ardent dedication. The type of man to slap backs and shout accolades, my boss presented me as an example more than once: of diligence, of flexibility, of growth. I learned early of his legendary temper, but rarely did he turn it on me. Indeed, his appreciation seemed genuine – if only for my cowering subordination.

Thankfully, what could've been seen as bootlicking was accepted as genuine by my workmates. I had a "friendly face," I was told. A refreshing energy – "especially for a Jew."

I was a lucky man. My future looked bright.

GATHER

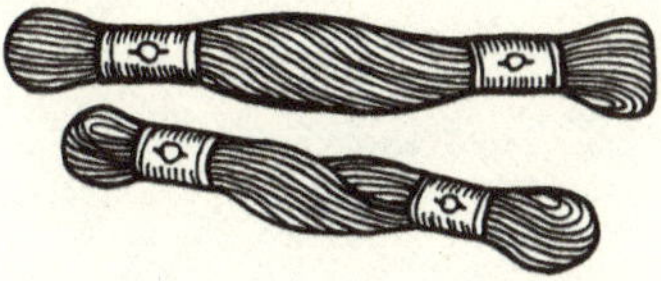

IN THE AUTUMN of 1925, I went to a nightclub. I wore nothing that revealed my background, but knew well it came through in other ways. My accent, for one, was hardly lessened by alcohol – though my tongue most certainly loosened. Unaccustomed to liquor, I was eager to learn, and hoped to undo a few assumptions in the process. While I wasn't the only Jewish man (or woman) at my work, I seemed to inspire something in my workmates that, shall we say, kept my heritage in the front of my mind.

The comments could be irksome, but none were threatening. In time, I'd use them as fuel, feeding a burning ambition, a blistering need to *prove* myself. Or at least beat others to the punch. If anyone was going to mock me – my health, my mannerisms, or my interests – it was going to be me. *I* would make people laugh, so help me God, at my own expense if necessary. The last thing I needed was friction in the office. Reliant as I was on the kindness of others, groveling might've been all I had between another bout of illness and unemployment. But I had my mother's humor to work with: dry, dark, and absurd. Adding it to my arsenal could only help.

Not everyone raised my defenses, though. I found a decent set with whom I could drop my guard, and used them as a social buffer as much as possible. A motley bunch from all different sectors, at work and otherwise, they were some of the most unusual people I'd ever met. Artists and writers, bohemians and flappers, Jews, Christians, atheists, even a self-proclaimed *spiritualist* (and *would I like a tarot reading?*). One man, fulfilling my own fantasy, was even known to wear jewelry – though, mind you, never before sunset.

It was these "freaks" (as they respectfully called themselves) who took me out that autumn eve. And while I can't remember anyone's name, I acutely recall the sense of leaning into them, timidly trying to untangle their jargon, to glean whatever wisdom they'd gained without me. They knew one another well, along with a broad circle of painters, singers, and top-caliber designers they felt I'd fit right in with. Their cryptic, coy comments seemed to indicate some latent talent I'd yet to discover in myself. Another hidden potential I was the last to find. I simply struck them as *that way*.

I took it as a compliment.

I'd only gone to one or two pubs before, and never to a club like this. I usually went straight home after work, but felt it was high time I bond with my colleagues. Unorthodox in appearance, their club of choice boasted dim booths, a hideous rug, and a handful of tables peppered over a dance floor. My memories are strange, though. Dreamlike. Floating lamps over a cavernous hall, the bar stretching on interminably – everything's gone curvy in death. Distorted. Upended and cast off to sail those shadowy, rippling voids in the continuum.

There were dozens of people there, though there was plenty of room for more. It must have been midweek. At that age, I stayed home on Friday and Saturday. My relationship with Shabbos hadn't yet undergone my "reformation" – though the change began that very night.

I wasn't concerned when my workmates wandered off and left me. I was on my third drink – meaning I was solidly drunk – and supervised by a stranger I'd deemed the most trustworthy in all of London. His eyes were hazel and crinkled when he smiled, his hair was the color of sand. Dimpled and breezy, he sat calm and collected while I leaned against the bar, regaling him with my typical routine of self-deprecating jokes.

And then he interrupted me: "Why would you say such things?" A voice so rich and honeyed, I can taste it still. "Show yourself some respect!"

His name was Peter Barnett. Or at least I think it was. But to admit I've lost even *his* name, to open such a ghastly chasm – I refuse. He's too solid, still, too real: sitting there, chin in hand, thoughtfully smirking.

I never did deserve him.

And yet listen to me! Clinging to and hoarding every tiny crumb of a memory. Trapping him – trapping both of us – knowing full well that unless I let go neither of us will be free. Unless I release that man, we're both prisoners.

I just don't know how.

His name, I repeat, was Peter Barnett. He was born on March 8, 1903.

He bought me two drinks that night, and all he asked in return was that I be kind to myself.

THIMBLE

IT WAS PETER who finally laid to rest the specter of *Reuben.* His regard for authenticity was powerful, religious even, and he found it sad that I'd hide who I was born to be. There would always be those who called me Reuben, of course, if only from sheer laziness, but I stopped encouraging it – and Peter launched a veritable campaign against the so-called "Reubenites."

He called me Ruvi. Family alone called me Ruvi.

I took to meeting Peter for coffee. Always midday, during work hours. A proud Cambridge dropout, he'd eschewed academia in favor of journalism, conducting interviews and writing critical reviews of art and theater, music and opera. He was on the up and up. A man about town. In with the in-crowd. Able to drop an awful lot of names.

But when we were together, none of that mattered.

My sole concern was making him laugh.

He had it in him – such a beautiful, full, glistening laugh – but it took effort to draw it out. I could say almost anything, turn the world upside down, stare into his eyes, unblinking, until my corneas burned

– and still I'd be the one cracking. But the ice was slowly melting. He was the one who kept asking me out, after all. And each time I saw him, he seemed more relaxed. A little stupider. A little more prone to blushing.

But he was awfully reserved at first. Confoundingly British.

He had good reason, though. It was chilling, hearing him speak of his family. I struggled to imagine the things he'd disclose, so different from my own tender upbringing – but it was hardly the only time my naïvety was spotlighted by Peter Barnett. It was a slow realization, how sheltered I'd been, and not just on account of my health. Nor was it youth, religion, or even the self-circling habits of immigrant life. No: my whole worldview had been astoundingly skewed by the simple fact that I'd come from a caring home.

Few myths are more pervasive than that of the loving family – a near-impossible illusion to break unless you're raised with its antithesis. And even then. Peter himself only seemed half-aware of how cruel his parents were, even as he recounted their clashes. It was like he found their treatment of him warranted. Like it was normal. Like abuse was love.

The problem, in his eyes, was him. His ruthless detection, criticism, and attempts to reform the corruptions he saw at home and in society. His utter inability to leave well enough alone.

But wasn't that exactly the best of him?

His icy mother just couldn't see it, nor could his

vainglorious sister. And his father and grandmother, despite their successes, weren't half as bright as he was. As far as I was concerned, his whole extended family – a cult of prestige more occupied with *looking* good than *being* good – simply felt threatened by him. By his keen eye, dissecting their habits. His intrepid mind, probing the parallels of private and public iniquity. His warm heart, ever striving to make things better.

But I wasn't afraid.

In fact, I couldn't get enough.

Never had I met someone whose thirst for truth matched my own, and Peter's undoubtedly exceeded it. He crusaded against injustice: all the prejudice, turpitude and poverty he simply *couldn't not see*. And how mournful it made him! How frustrated, how lonely. So often crushed by his own self-doubt. Young, sweet, earnest Peter: my hopeless humanist, as committed to equality as I was to making him a buffoon.

I just couldn't stand to see him sad.

I'd seen the silliness he was capable of, the facetious absurdity pressing against the walls, desperate to escape – and nothing had ever charmed me so much in my life. It shook awake a version of me I'd never known: a weird and wild thing, a child of a most surreal nature. We became each other's projects, as well as rivals – the fool and the philosopher, intellectual adversaries in a farcical play, wielding fits of hysteria so consuming that in the end neither was the victor.

Good God, I was in love.

It was swift. It was total. It was irreversible. Whatever I'd been before wilted and died and a whole new species bloomed in its place: a compulsively affectionate, mildly feverish, insufferably cheeky devil. Just like Peter. Each time we met, we sat a little closer. Spoke a little stranger. Touched a little longer. I would've spent every second with him, arm in arm, drunk with laughter, frankly disturbing the peace – but I had work, a home in Stamford Hill, and, inexplicably, a rather austere religious life.

And, of course, I also had asthma.

It was a lengthy flare-up that first drew Peter to my house. He knew my address. He knew many things about me by then, yet I'm not sure I'd mentioned my condition. I found it embarrassing (among other things) and avoided the topic if I could, especially with those I admired. A laughable ploy, of course; it was hardly a keepable secret. Two months had passed since our first meeting, and autumn was fast becoming winter – arguably my hardest season. Anything could do me in, if I'm honest: the sweetness of spring, the oppression of summer. Perfume. Dog hair. Night. But chimney smoke and smog, frigid air and London's "fog" – that could knock me down for weeks.

And it wasn't getting easier. I'd put my lungs first for years, bending my whole life to suit their whims. I'd pampered them, listened intently to their complaints, showered them with attention. But I'd lost my taste for prioritizing them. Next to Peter, they were decidedly second place.

And they got jealous.

I'm sure my family was confused by this goy on their doorstep, standing in the rain, asking to talk to their bedridden son. But they let him in, and that's all that mattered to me.

I remember how stricken he was by my appearance: muttering about blue lips, looking like he wanted to go. Whatever he'd planned to say had lost significance. After a brief, uneasy exchange, he left my room to talk to my parents – leaving me dejected. Ashamed of my weakness. But I needn't have worried; Peter had made it clear, after all, that helping the needy was his top priority.

I was in a twilight state – sunk by the naval battle between breathlessness and sleep – when he returned, kissed my forehead, ruffled my hair, and told me he'd be back in the morning.

My parents had agreed for him to take me away.

It was certainly unprecedented. Perhaps Peter had promised them something. Or perhaps they were simply tired of me. At the time, I didn't give it (or anything) much thought. It was Peter, Peter Barnett, so I went with him: from a cab to a rail car to another cab. He brought me coffee and read aloud. He let me rest on his shoulder.

I'd make that trip countless times over the years, almost always under the same circumstances. But it's fuzzy now, in this annihilating nebula. This deafening solitude. How long has it been, anyway? I'd guess I've been dead for twice as long as I was ever alive.

At least. But time matters no more here than it did on those dreamlike train rides. Even when Peter got his own car, those drives were no more coherent from the back seat. Semiconscious and smothered, those memories never stood a chance.

I like to imagine the first time I woke, well and alert at the end of that ordeal. I picture myself in that large bed, clear-headed and curious, drinking fresh, salty air through the open window. Peter coming in with a smile. The nervous glow, knowing we're alone.

But I'm making it all up.

Honestly, I can't tell one trip from the next. It's all a blur: a fifteen-year smear of health-crises and holidays. Asthma casting its crooked spells. Accidental blessings. Collateral miracles. Getting me out of the city, away from the smog, to the sea, to the sea – that was the goal. Where it was clean, where I could recover. In a little white cottage up a thin road, tucked between wide-spaced houses and gardens and sheds – just a sliver of water in sight. Two bedrooms and a quaint little kitchen, flooded with antiques and heirlooms and maritime kitsch. A chest of musty blankets. A cast iron stove. A golden telescope.

The house was called Shorehaven: a haven among havens, with Newhaven, Peacehaven, and Seaford mere minutes away. It belonged to Peter's parents, and we used it without their awareness or consent. It was meant for Peter's brother, Richard. Older than us, Rich had fought in the war, and he never quite stopped. Alarmed by the change in their shell-shocked son, the Barnetts repurposed an old cottage for his recovery. But he found less healing there than I did. Ultimately, he grew distant, vanishing up north – breaking Peter's heart in the process.

I did what I could to bring light to those dark corners. Peter had given me a means to mend, after all, and I intended to return the favor.

We'd venture into Seaford as soon as I was able – prowling grassy cliffs, rocky beaches, and local pubs. Over beers we'd tease strangers, challenging them to games, arm-wrestling matches, all kinds of dares. We'd toy with reality, posing as time travelers, actors, circus members, even mythological creatures – egging each other on with prompts and accents and (at least once) costumes. We were free in our anonymity. Sizzling and electric, high on one another. Bottling ludicrous letters and casting them out to sea, we were hardly able to recognize ourselves.

I'm sure we were terribly annoying to be around.

Thankfully, most of our time was spent alone: lazy hours by the waves, below the phantom watch of the Seven Sisters, lost in talk that almost deserves to be forgotten. We never needed words, really. We were cut from the same fabric, he and I, meant from the start to be sewn back together. All our petty differences – our views and our histories, our status in society – they only served to keep it interesting. Embroidery on the voile, giving us something to ponder while enjoying the elegance and comfort of how well we *fit.*

From that very first trip, we were making love. Clumsy, desperate love, in all sorts of imaginative ways.

I can't recall our first touch, but the aching, grasping, mindless abandon stayed with me. The warmth of his body, the hunger of his lips. And the inescapable comedy, even in the heat of passion – laughing as we fumbled, joking as we kissed, humored by our hidden similarities. Feeling good, for once. Safe in my own skin. I came down from my cloud, into my body, and forgot completely why I'd ever left.

It wasn't blind lust, though. It was the only logical thing in the world. We simply *had* to be close. Closer and closer and closer. We were one, in the end: one mind, one heart, one purpose in life. To be separate, divided in any way – *that* was the crime against nature. Earthly rules simply didn't apply. Together, we were cosmic.

Love like that could only be divine, ordained by God Himself. A force for healing, a force for good. A force for so much more than Peter and me alone. My hands were God's hands; through me, God loved Peter, and through *us* God would love the world. I knew it with the ineffable certainty of a prophet. All sin was burned clean by that fire. Guilt and shame and self-consciousness: ash in the embers of sacred blessing. The God I knew, the God I'd once met in the throes of death, would not condemn this. My God would not rob me of breath – my neshama, my very soul – then give such sublimity only to test my will. After all the work I'd done to stay alive – the exhausting, agonizing labor of treading water all those years – this was my payoff. My reward.

I wasn't drowning anymore. I'd finally found the shore.

I passed us through every ethical filter I could contrive, and the results were always the same: I'd do far more damage by resisting this than giving into it. With Peter in my arms, I could end wars; without him, I might very well start them.

I can only imagine the thrill Peter got from it, having me in that bed – the very bed his parents slept in on holiday. Me, of all people: a Jew, a foreigner, a *man*. He didn't hide the malicious glee he felt. The horror his family would suffer should they ever find out! I knew I was a weapon in his battle.

But I also knew I was more than that.

This was more than that.

This was milk and this was honey. This was God's work on Earth. This was *beshert.*

And thus began the rest of my life: an ephemeral oscillation of extremes. Pleasure and pain. Lust and piety. Work and play. Laughter and dread.

London and Seaford.

PRESS

IN 1926, PETER and I moved in together. Significant funds were cut when Peter's family learned just who his new flatmate was to be, but we managed with our own resources. I'm sure the Barnetts expected a brief tenure: merely another act of rebellion by their most wayward son. No one anticipated how entrenched we'd become, least of all the two of us. But no home could've met our needs better. Our tiny flat in Shepherd Market offered an easy walk to work, a web of cozy strolls, and countless remedies for our restlessness: parks, Piccadilly, and close proximity to Soho's scene and international cuisine.

Plus, neither of us wanted to move the piano back down three flights of stairs.

Living with Peter quelled the myriad withdrawal symptoms I suffered in his absence and, while it brought no relief to other ailments, I felt safe sleeping next to him – even when I woke up suffocating. I'm sure my mother was happy to hand me off. Long gone were her nights of singing and sock darning at my bedside, but the fact remained that no one slept well unless I did.

Consequently, not much was said to dissuade

me from moving. Merely the quotidian compulsions of good Jewish parents: there was no lift (could I *manage*?), it was rather dreary (needed a woman's touch), and, most curiously, the flat only had one bedroom. They offered to chip in for a bigger place, perhaps in a different neighborhood, but we assured them this was temporary. Step one toward independence. Peter could sleep on the sofa.

Somehow, they were convinced, and remarkably unsuspecting – my mother, especially. Over the years, she was given plenty of cause to question our ruse, but she didn't. In fact, I think she chose not to. Her brain became a labyrinth of pretext, where any touches were "brotherly" and overheard pet names innocent banter. Even sharing a bed was fair play to her: after all, it got cold at night.

My father, though. He likely came to guess. Try as I might, I could never shake the sense of being exposed around him: clothed in clear glass, braced for the impact of accusations, forever expecting to be cut by the shards. But he never said anything. Perhaps a mumbled remark now and then, a knowing unease in his tone. But nothing more. The sad truth is he never had much hope for me. That I was even gainfully employed was more than he'd expected. I'd always been strange in his eyes, and hopelessly sick. Finding me a bride likely hadn't crossed his mind. Who would want me for a husband? Who would have me?

Ada, on the other hand, was well on track to giving them grandchildren, which also took some pressure off me. Whether she'd wind up with a good

Jewish boy, however, remained up for debate. Not for the first time, my sister and I seemed to have the same taste.

My parents made a lot of accommodations for us. But as I've said, they were soft people. They let us be who we needed to be.

In spite of his doubts (or perhaps to make up for them), my father even made a place for Peter in his life. Their ethical interests paired well, as did their appetites for chess, and once that was discovered they got along swimmingly. In fact, at times I felt he preferred Peter – poised, strapping and whip-smart – to the delicate, peculiar son he'd been saddled with. It was as though I'd brought him a replacement. Peter was even welcome for Shabbos, so long as he made time for whatever game he had going with my father. They took it seriously. At times they'd get so lost in their match, I'd feel like an intruder.

Which was fine by me.

When my father was present, Peter and I took pains to put space between us. The man's offish glances made it clear he didn't share my mother's blind bliss. If word got out to his brothers on the Continent, the scandal would be ruinous. Our performance might've won over other audiences, but necessity made a harsh critic of my father. A quiet one, true, but nerve-rackingly keen.

I was well practiced, though; he wasn't the only person I performed for. My employer also preferred I keep up appearances, and I did everything in my power to appease him. My steady ascent up the ladder of success often left me winded, and the higher I climbed, the more breathless the pace. I was productive, though – indeed, so productive that my boss even let me work from the coast. It beat not working at all, he supposed, and apparently my contributions were "invaluable." Peter called it servitude, hardly above sweatshop labor – and he would know. His family had made their fortune running such places. Pained by the parallels, he urged me to cut my hours, or even seek work elsewhere, free from my boss's demanding moods. But my many needs kept me on edge. I was lucky to even be employed. Rectitude and competence became almost literally the air I breathed, flowing into every corner of my professional life – in stark contrast with more lackadaisical workmates. But their bronchial tubes weren't tied to their paychecks.

All the same, those workmates were among my very best friends.

They'd seen me all along for precisely what I was: a "freak," just like them. A lost child, a marooned alien. A pansy, completely unaware of its petals. And how charming they'd found my ignorance! It continued to be a source of humor for years. Attempting to counter this bias by sharing what I *did* know (theological theory) only further entrenched their views. My monochromatic past hadn't prepared me one bit for the headiness of modern London. Adding a *secret love cult* to the mix left me so adorably baffled that my cohorts all but fought over who'd get to initiate me.

They'd known exactly what they were doing at that club, the night they left me alone with Peter. They were conducting a test.

And I suppose I passed.

My relationship with Peter was rather renowned, in fact. An enviable romance to many – and to those who'd introduced us, a bit of a shock. They'd only aimed to out me; open my eyes to the possibilities. Instead, I mated for life, upending all future matchmaking schemes.

I wish I could tell you more about these fellows. Everyone was older, taller, and more thoroughly British than I was, that much is clear. Perhaps two or three were Jewish, but anglicized almost beyond recognition compared to what I'd known. In so many ways, I lived two separate lives, and they clashed like night and day.

And how night and day clashed!

From sunup to sundown, my colleagues passed as perfectly ordinary, but as soon as the moon rose they mutated, transformed by dinner and drinks into mythical monsters: supernatural creatures of gaiety, gossip, and romance.

Everyone had a sobriquet, and I remember those far better than proper names. Some were flung haphazardly, sticking to almost anyone in the room: *Mary*, *Fay*, *Rose*. Others were specific and personal, fabricated to shield against blackmail – or worse. Barons and bureaucrats were woven with our lot, married men with distinguished reputations. But most played with lower stakes. Peter was particularly open to this game. Despite his insistence that I embrace my birth name, he nursed a certain distaste for his own. Which was understandable enough; his parents often said it like a bad word.

Owing to my family's positive (if slightly bemused) reaction to Peter, it was only fair to introduce me to his relatives in turn. Two or three times, we attempted this: always outside, at backyard picnics or Kensington Gardens. Places without doors – yet, somehow, they'd manage to slam one in my face anyway. I can't recall ever speaking with these people, but I've no trouble dredging up their eyes on me: gathered in the shade, lounging on blankets, clad in checkers and pinstripes and white. Looking affronted.

I'm sure I was underdressed at these events. The clothing I wore favored comfort over fashion. My aversion to neckties and top buttons often set me apart, and I chronically neglected to polish my shoes. But that was no reason for Peter's grandmother to call me "the Jew boy."

Nor was it cause for that family to pretend I didn't exist.

Like synchronized dancers, they'd avoid all contact with me – including eye contact. To say I felt out of place would be an understatement. I felt like a corpse. A rotten body found by capricious chance in the bushes during a game of croquet. *Memento mori* in the flesh: such a shock to the senses that gala guests could only suffer my existence by turning away, holding their breath, waiting for someone to haul me off – and God, the sooner the better. To face me, even to stare as one might at a horrible accident, would too greatly damage the brain. Best to prevent the trauma.

But the worst part was watching Peter. Locked in a dance of his own, he'd dodge veiled insults, duck social curveballs, field unyielding and impractical demands framed as innocuous requests. The rules and customs I considered normal were all thrown out the window. Peter's character was determined not by his actions and ideas, but by whomever happened to be speaking at the moment – and the assessments were random, degrading, and baffling. It was they, not he, who chose his feelings. *They* declared what his thoughts were, and all efforts to reclaim his identity only invited derision. Peter would be backed into a corner, forced to comply and agree. Forced to humiliate himself. Anything less than complete surrender of autonomy was seen as rebellion. The simple act of saying "no" – even to a sandwich – qualified as insufferable arrogance. All attempts at self-expression, right down to an opinion on the weather: autocratic bickering. And woe upon Peter should he show any displeasure at this; the onus of hurt feelings fell squarely on the victim. How dare he always be so fussy?

Peter would change in this environment. No longer the funny, gentle intellectual I'd fallen for, he'd grow anxious and self-conscious, reactionary and confused. And who could blame him? These people had claws, talons tearing deep into his mind. Their erosion of common sense would weaken anyone's sanity, and they convinced Peter to take full blame for his frazzled state. More often than not, he'd end up with a migraine.

It wasn't hard to see how he'd grown from this. That family was a boot camp. A training ground for extraordinary perceptions. Peter's brilliance was built navigating this. His uncanny awareness of ulterior motives: a survival mechanism. The stunning complexity of his social critiques: a lotus in the mud. And his desire, his all-consuming need to *fix* things – alleviate suffering, overthrow the oppressor, uplift the downtrodden – was a natural consequence of feeling the sting himself. An environment so toxic could only produce two things: genius or insanity.

Or perhaps more abuse.

For that's exactly what this was: unambiguous abuse. Even without the physical violence he'd also endured, I knew what I was looking at. Peter never quite saw it, though. For all his acuity, he never did grasp how much those people hurt him, nor that he'd done nothing to deserve it.

And for that, I loved him all the more fiercely. Perhaps the contrast would help.

I soon gave up trying to meet his family, but abandoning "Project Barnett" (as we'd dubbed it) didn't spare me their judgments. Peter would return from visits distraught, disgusted by slurs he'd heard about me – and I'd beg him to keep it to himself. I imagined such things were said behind *many* closed doors, not just his parents' – but I benefited little from having my suspicions confirmed.

I was an optimist, after all. Strange as that is to say now.

Peter withdrew from them in time, but never fully removed himself. We lived in relative ease, though; chances of a surprise visit were next to none. Peter's sister appeared only once, bearing a large bouquet from some family event, but wouldn't dare set foot in our "ridiculous squalor." Peter's refusal of the flowers spurred a tirade from the woman, concerns for my allergies twisted into thankless self-absorption. In the end, she tossed the flowers at his feet. I remember well my shock (and undeniable arousal) when Peter opened a window and threw them back at her as she left the building.

I don't know what Peter did, in any lifetime, to deserve such a family, but I can't claim they have no utility. The cure for naïvety is knowing deception, after all. I've said it before: you can't learn without a lesson. If I stand any chance of breaking my bad habits and not repeating all the damning, misguided mistakes I've made, I'd do well to find a family like that. Learn something new, give my next life some purpose.

I can't stay like this forever. I have to face the music eventually.

NOTIONS

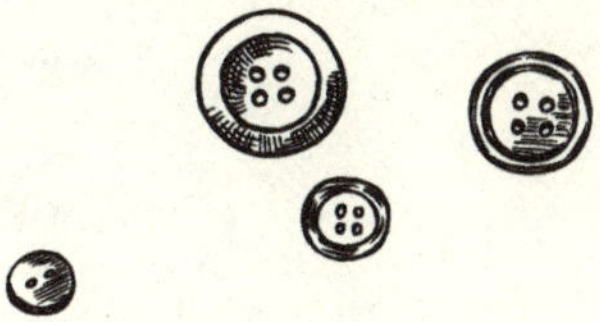

ON THE TOPIC of music, I was never the best at it. I could manage piano alright, and (voice permitting) I wasn't afraid to sing. But music was Peter's forte, and not just compared to me. He was serious about it, and practiced almost daily – knuckles having taken too much rapping to renounce his skills. His childhood followed him just as closely as anyone's. He took requests when I was ill, and it's a testament to music's immortality that I still can't tell if Satie's Gnossiennes bring me comfort or a breathless sense of doom. His family called on him as well, exploiting his talents in formal shows I (clearly) never attended. His mastery of piano seemed the only thing his parents liked about him. To put it plainly: it was easy to flaunt.

But Peter also played guitar. He'd picked it up as a form of rebellion, and, as one might expect, used it mainly for protest songs. He collected them from around the globe – anthems for workers and women and revolutions – and sang them giggling, fumbling any foreign language but French. He barely even knew Yiddish, despite the ranting I was given to under stress, and his grasp of Hebrew was no greater than mine as a child: he simply liked the sound. He could feel the meaning, though. He could feel *everything* – deeply and soulfully, and it came out in his music. In the poetry he wrote, in the verses he read, in the melodious tremor of his golden voice. A voice like butter and honey and bourbon. A summer sunset on a glistening pond. A voice I never grew tired of.

Unlike my own. Wounded by coughs and prone to mystifying maladies, my voice frequently performed a mysterious vanishing act. One doctor guessed it was psychosomatic: a phobia of speaking with such a "troublesome" accent. Needless to say, I found a new doctor. I'd long since overcome my self-consciousness. With Peter by my side, I sang as often as I could, and Peter never complained.

No one did, in fact – and an awful lot of people, by the end of my life, would hear us sing.

Like Peter, I never fully outgrew my roots, nor could I escape the leaves and branches. Should I be caught in bad company, the whole family tree could be poisoned. So I generally avoided clubs, eschewing the drag balls my friends frequented – but was never one to pass on a good house party. In fact, I became a veritable bacchant, drinking to the point of song whenever I was able. We enjoyed increasingly upscale events, put on by actors and musicians Peter met through his work, and fellow artists in my own field – including virtual celebrities. To strangers, Peter presented me like a gem, giving me confidence to take the social reins when he inevitably dropped them, worn down by hours of small talk. A stiff drink and a side of self-effacing humor carried me through any starstruck stumbling; over time I learned I could rub elbows with just about anyone.

Yet to call these "parties" hardly does them justice. They were living animals in their own right, multidimensional beings at their peak, adorned with costumes and jewels, showcasing innumerable talents. Guests gave bawdy performances, hilarious and extraordinary. From the comfort of an armchair, I was privy to everything one could find at a nightclub: burlesques, contortionist acts, and endless musical entertainment, all put on by curious acquaintances, respected colleagues, and dear friends. These affairs usually came to a somber close, with a heartfelt recital of poetry or a particularly sad song. The audience would boo, complain, or succumb to teary-eyed reverie – roughly dependent on how much liquor had been consumed.

It was there that Peter and I shined. A shared passion for theater made us adept with song and dance, and we concocted uproarious sketches involving both. Though never longer than five or ten minutes, our skits were filled to the brim with riveting drama, romance, and comedy. We'd practice at home some, but between the papers in Peter's office (the dining room), the books piled in the library (the bedroom), and the fabric scraps of my sewing nook (everywhere else), there was hardly space for a two-step. For that, we found another remedy in Shorehaven. Along with its curative coastal air, the house's sparse furnishings, antique piano, and quaint, coin-slot gramophone gave it boundless medicinal value. There we could play and dance and test our crass lyrics, cooking up little shows in our increasingly melded mind. Spinning round and into each other like eggs and flour in a mixing bowl. Tastier together than apart.

The results were lauded. We were honored guests, met with enthusiasm when we came to the door. Never mind Peter's rum-soaked political rants or my incurable quirks. And never mind *us*, odd pairing that we were, in our bizarre and exclusive whimsy. We'd be drunk on one another long before the alcohol got us, speaking a language all our own. But no one seemed to mind our behavior. In fact, people drew to us like moths to flame: learning our games, playing along, even adopting my made-up words – my sloppy butchering of English – as slang. Our love gave off a "glow," we were told. A warmth that others could gather round. A paragon of the heart's potential. A rare example of purity.

Healing and divine, just as I suspected.

Peter scoffed at these claims, dismissing my mystical schmaltz as a misguided attempt to *justify* us. When I'd "take to the clouds," he'd feign brushing them away – comically waving me down when I flew too high. I was allowed to simply love, he'd remind me. To enjoy life, for my own sake. I needn't make religious excuses. "Clear that smoke from your eyes, Ruvi. You'll end up with an asthma attack."

His protests were hollow, though. I knew he felt it, all the same. Like a lock and key, we let in something bigger than either of us. In our own strange way, we repaired the world.

Dancing, singing, and sacred love; I'd somehow become a triple threat.

Peter took his aspirations further still, even trying his hand at scriptwriting (albeit to little avail). I provided feedback and helped him edit, but ultimately it was his project. His unrealized dream. Eroded by the criticism of his family, he ended up discouraged. Depressed and insecure, he threw his writing away.

And what a loss. It's such a sacred thing, writing. A holy craft: forging form from letters like God Himself. And Peter was always so careful with his words. Intentional. Honest. Wise. I imagine it was heartbreaking.

But I can't quite remember.

It feels so long ago. Like a dream. Like it never happened at all.

And who's to say it did? I haven't any proof – no artifacts, no documents or witnesses. Who's to say it isn't pure delusion? Myth, forgery. I never deserved love or family or friendship – none of it. Who am I kidding? I'm air and water, a cloud, a treacherous mist of selfish longing. What nefarious deceit, claiming I existed at all! In a body. In a community. Imagining hands, like I'd use them for good. Like I could make beauty. Imaging I *belonged*! That's no more than the desperate musing of a lonely ghost.

One thing still convinces me, though. One small but compelling piece of evidence: that relentless burn – like a molten ribbon – tying me to the living, tangling me in my crimes. That thin channel of pain, narrow as my vision, twisted as my logic, long as . . . well . . . I suppose my memory. A scar that searing simply wouldn't be there without cause.

Perhaps doubt itself is holding me here. If I could only commit and believe that *yes*, these stories are mine, then perhaps I could find the key, the door, and the long hall back out of this place. Clear that ghastly, resonant note from my mind. Silence that echoing shot. Otherwise, how can I fix what I've done? I can't hide here forever, trapped by my own uncertainty, while my every living relative bears the mark of my shame.

I can't beat myself up when others feel the punches.

I need to leave this place.

EASE

I'M SORRY. I lost it for a second, didn't I? That happens sometimes. I swear, my thoughts were never this frazzled before the Blitz.

But we're not there yet, are we? Whether any of this is true or not, it can't be later than 1935.

Anna was alive by then. Little Annie, my niece. Born in 1930, in February. I remember because it was only seven months after my sister's wedding – and she wasn't premature.

Edwin came a few years later.

I loved being an uncle. I should've focused on that more. I should've focused on family, on London, on art and beauty and God. Instead, I focused only on myself.

The '30s were mostly a good time, though. The Great Slump didn't hurt us any. Quite the opposite, in fact. Peter's work mushroomed ever outward, assignments now encompassing Hollywood, enabling him (on rare occasion) to interview a true star.

He took up a side gig, as well, albeit quietly: writing and editing for a socialist magazine.

My own job also evolved – granting more opportunities to sew, to create, to style models and mannequins for fashion shows and department store displays. A return to my teen years, in a way. Once more on the floor, pins in mouth, eyes tired from squinting (even after getting glasses). But the fabric was finer, the linens softer, embellishments diaphanous and dreamy. I still drew, of course. I always drew. It was all I could do from Shorehaven, after all, and Shorehaven only took more and more of my time.

My asthma was increasingly unwelcome at the office. One emergency was one too many.

My heart stopped on a Monday: March 5, 1934. A senseless slaughter, really. In my quest for belonging, untimely illness had come to feel like failure. Pride, not for the first time, waved away help until it was too late. Drowned at my desk with no medication, I traumatized my workmates – yet somehow, just as in childhood, I emerged unscathed.

Better than ever, in fact.

For the second time, death worked its magic: loosing me from my brittle cage to soar about the heavens. Like a brilliant, sanitizing mikveh, it purified me. Restored me. *Reminded* me. In surreal, celestial visions, I was shown behind the veil – the labyrinth of our lives, twisted paths we forge ourselves – and returned to the ecstasy of faith. The bliss of inspiration. The uncompromising certainty of love. Senses enlivened, I was attuned to the wondrous delicacy hidden all around: beauty, beauty, beauty in all things.

I would've done well, ultimately, to let nature

take its course. I clearly had the impulse to fly away, otherwise I wouldn't have kept doing it. But the body has to be as willing as the mind, I suppose. Taking matters into my own hands certainly didn't end well.

Not that nature's always easy.

Resurrected in an ambulance, I returned to life tender. Porous, ethereal, otherworldly, almost unrecognizable – and you know how humans react to the unknown. How they cling to logic, the mirage of materialism, to their own amnesia like a child with a blanket, fighting any attempt to do the laundry. It's not wrong, of course: the scope and convolution of reality could easily break the fragile mind. It's hard enough to keep your head, especially in this world. I've certainly known more sensible places. I learned fast to keep enlightenment to myself. If it isolated me as a child, it outright ostracized me as an adult – raising questions, stirring concerns. Not even Peter wanted to hear about it; it simply made him sad. The frailty of my existence troubled him enough without my eccentric reminders.

I couldn't ignore it, though, nor did I want to. I held onto those visions – motivating, intoxicating, and true – for as long as I could. It almost seemed that God was *teaching* me something: doggedly repeating some esoteric lesson in hopes that I'd share what I'd learned. Use it to help others. But I couldn't quite decode the message, and worse still, no one would listen. The weight of revelation soon grew too heavy. I lost my grip and let it fall. Sunk in a subliminal swamp, it mingled with my other secrets and quietly began my undoing.

My return to work was celebrated: drinks and sweets first thing in the morning. It occurred to no one, least of all me, that I might be unfit for employment. I could've easily lived on Peter's salary, sparing him undue stress in the process, but let's face it: I was vain. My professional reputation trumped everything. A semblance of success, the illusion of strength, a steady income – these I'd placed above all else. I was quite literally willing to die for money.

And I'm sure that's coming back to bite me. There's no way around revisiting views like that.

It wasn't exactly greed, though. The goal was never to get more. It was to *be* more: more than an immigrant, more than a Jew, more than – God forbid – whatever else people assumed about me. If I wanted acceptance, I simply had to perform. If I wanted respect, I had to dance that dance.

But you know how I loved dancing.

Truly, I relished what I did. I was designing my own patterns now, not just depicting those of others. I'd been granted one of my greatest wishes: to do for the world what I'd once done for Ada. Or at least to do it for London.

My job took me all throughout the city, affording me new and interesting views. Less time at drafting tables, more time at shows and shops, at warehouses and bazaars – examining textiles, scrutinizing them, rubbing them against my cheek. Loving them, almost as I loved Peter. I had an eye for detail, I was told again and again. I made my living on detail. I could smell quality, taste a bargain, sense the popularity of colors and prints as they rose and fell like tides. With a single touch, I could know a thread count.

I was sensitive, after all, and all the more so after a taste of death: to minutia, to emotion, to the needs of others. To the resonant pitch and tone of my office. Of England. Of the rapidly changing world.

Probably too sensitive. I couldn't even stomach the news.

But it paid the bills, and then some. I had plenty of savings. Beyond my growing medical expenses, I led a frugal life. Following my father's lead, I sent some of my earnings to the Continent, to family in Holland and Belgium and Poland, just as they'd once done for us. And along with Peter, I donated to several charities. I could finally give back after so much taking. I could finally balance the scales.

I'd become a man. Highly esteemed, commended for my taste. Trusted, respected, and in demand. A force to reckon with until five o'clock – and otherwise living in pajamas.

In our off time, Peter and I carried on in private reverie: feeding alley cats, befriending statues, mythologizing the world. We never moved from Shepherd Market. Instead, its narrow veins became our own. Our little flat: a shared limb. Our mingled thoughts, externalized in paper stacks and crooked book towers: souvenirs from untold flights of fancy. Lazy days were spent dreaming in Green Park, lulled by the lullaby of bleating sheep. And nights were given to cinema, to Fred and Ginger and diligent studies of their footwork. Our life was simple. Tucked away, protected and safe. We huddled like birds in an aerie, high above the street – preening and singing, laughing and dancing, reading aloud. Wasting hours upon hours in bed.

I made most of our clothes, though there were a few prized items from elsewhere. Bespoke suits, imported gloves. And shoes! How Peter loved his shoes – owned nearly a dozen pairs, and polished them constantly. I only had a couple, and they would've remained scuffed were it not for Peter's attentions. His propriety overflowed – adjusting my collars, smoothing my hair, keeping me just as presentable as he was. And teasing me all the while: how little I understood such things! How did I ever get my job? How lucky I was to have him.

Yet Peter's decorum did not spill evenly. Our home, simply put, was a mess. A beautiful, artful, sacred, fertile, almost intentional mess – but a mess. A snarl of fabric and ink, boxes for a coffee table, three typewriters, and a wardrobe "with a leak." But still, we'd have friends over – some of the same crowd that attended those luxurious galas where we put on our shows. Our own get-togethers were never very big, of course, on account of the space, but they were no less eclectic. I remember candlelit dinners on the floor, miniature concerts and singalongs, whimsical games of wordplay, and even a séance: a failed but earnest attempt to contact our friend Ferdie.

Ferdie was the house ghost. The third flatmate. *Ferdinand*, we called him – though I have no idea why.

His knocks and footsteps were common, but bearable. Less tolerable were the movements: shifting objects, slamming doors, dishes flying from shelves. Even Peter's clothes were torn. Cut, perhaps – a whole shirt in pieces, with no explanation. Things disappeared as well: clothing, keys, sketches, money. We blamed the ghost for missing items whether it was his fault or not – sparing us many an unneeded argument. It wasn't entirely fair, given that Ferdie was there first. But we tried to make it up to him. We'd invite him to tea. Include him in conversation, ask about his day. Offer up a drink on those rare, chilling occasions when we heard him weep. We kept an uneasy peace.

In truth, however, despite all this, I wasn't sure I believed in ghosts back then. They just didn't fit with my view of death. Can you imagine? The irony!

By the end, I'd be little more than a ghost myself.

I was happy, though, for years and years. Cradled in a romantic, bohemian peace. I kept the same flamboyant friends, with their weekend wigs and clip-on earrings. I kept the same employer. And I kept on loving Peter – desperately, at times, for I knew it couldn't last. My dance with death only deepened my faith in us: the sanctity of our connection, the godliness of our bond. Restraining affection grew increasingly difficult, but I kept it tucked away, along with so much of my inner world. Secure in our nest, our hidden retreat, we merged in mutual esoterism. In our co-woven web of myth, we protected one another: from Peter's family, from Peter's guilt, from all his doubts and melancholy. From my weariness and wariness and periodic panic, from the dreaded instability of my days. Peter alone was my confidant, the sole sounding board for both my eccentricities and my conservatism. With him I rebelled against my past, and with him I indulged it – enjoying religious debates that would bore the wild world I'd somehow joined. Sharing the euphoria of constant creation, imbibing of God with each and every breath. Sharing the sorrows of earthly life. With him, I had Chopin, Bowlly, and Yiddisher jazz in equal measure. With him, I was all of me.

And, mostly, I stayed the same.

Only my eyes showed the passage of time, requiring lenses that gave me the distinct appearance of an owl. Turns out, those fanciful clouds Peter saw in my vision were *real* – and he took endless delight in reminding me of this. By my thirtieth birthday, I had two separate prescriptions; I couldn't see things far away any better than those right in front of me.

And if that's not a metaphor for my life, I don't know what is.

Annie and Edwin, though – my niece and nephew – they made a difference.

Ada was married at only eighteen, to a toe-headed, blue-eyed goy. My parents swallowed their pride and celebrated, overlooking their son-in-law's schooling (secular), religion (rugby), and even turning a blind eye to the suspicious timing of their granddaughter's birth – happy to have at least one of their children wed.

I was the one who took issue with these things.

Even after my brush with death – or perhaps because of it – Ada's choices rubbed me raw. With all her brilliance and potential, I loathed seeing her dim to suit a convenient marriage. Minor complaints, at first, but they would mutate, fermenting in my oxygen-deprived mind as time took what little remained of my breath. Ultimately, I'd learn just how hypocritical I could be.

But for years, my objections slumbered. I liked my brother-in-law, shallow though I found him; he was playful and light-hearted, nicely balancing Ada's solemnity. Contagiously spry, when he was around I'd get a bit rowdy myself.

But that could also be explained by the children.

Annie and I were instant friends. I vividly recall when first we met, in the parlor of my sister's quaint suburban home. She'd just woken from a nap when Ada placed her on my lap: three kilograms of strange, squirming warmth. It was less awkward than I'd expected, though I'd rarely held a baby, much less a newborn. She blinked at me curiously with amphibian eyes, broad and swollen and glossy. Breath like honey, cheeks like plums, soft and rare as vicuña wool. I went weak. A void was filled that I hadn't even been aware of – a pain I'd grown so used to, I thought it was normal. *This*, though. *This* is what I'd been missing. This tiny little creature. This almost edible hug.

She grew quickly, as people do, revealing a strong personality that only cast me deeper under her spell. She'd inherited her mother's sharp mind and dark hair – often worn in messy braids, for she'd also acquired her father's zest and penchant for grass stains. Playing with her was the most exercise I typically got, and that's saying nothing about my health. She was a firecracker. Not even Peter – college rower and avid swimmer – could keep up.

I took every opportunity to be around her, barring those near water. I simply couldn't bear it. Seeing her at a railing, looking down at a lake – it was enough to throw me into hysterics, plunged under completely.

Slip.

Gone.

But I treasured our time on solid ground.

I'm afraid I don't remember Edwin quite as well. He was several years younger, and largely lost with the wreckage of my mind. I vaguely recall his chubby, ruddy face. A bookish temperament. A certain shyness. But little more.

Annie, however. All pranks and puckishness. She'd dress me up and paint my face, pull me under the dining table and rope me into elaborate ploys. Even as my rapport with her mother unraveled, my bond with her remained firm. We loved each other, genuinely, in a way I really should've taken more seriously. But I had work, and I had Peter. I had society and politics and disease. Heartbreaking though it is to admit, Annie was just a small part of my life. I had no idea how big I was in hers. No idea that I was her world.

Perhaps things would've been different had I understood. But it's too late now.

צחוק

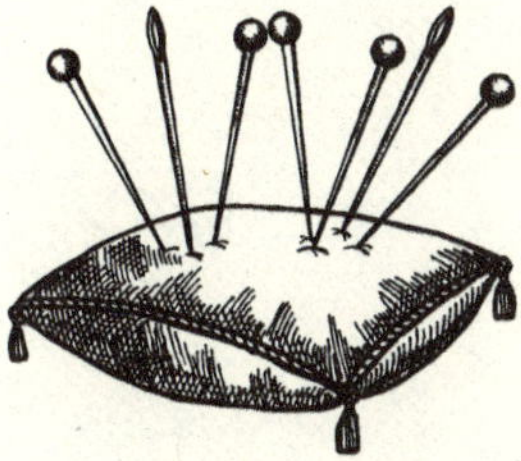

AROUND THE END of 1937, I broke.

I can't remember how or why it started, but it went on and on and on.

And no one seemed to grasp how *physical* it was. In a maddening confusion of cause and effect, friends blamed stress. My parents, fatigue from overwork. Metaphors came up, from the Shmita to my sex life, and Peter even dared to preach metaphysics, going so far as to suggest psychic wizardry. I was picking up on the drama in Germany, he guessed, poisoned by the mounting tension in the air. Perhaps all that God had shown me, unveiling His love in the transcendence of death, had "thinned the walls" a bit too much. Perhaps I was even more sensitive than I thought.

I see now that Peter wasn't wrong – that all life shares one beating heart, and through it I could feel and express the woes of the collective without realizing. But at the time I didn't know – and if I'd had the strength then, I would have murdered him.

Weeks would pass without a break from my asthma. The flare-ups would expand and contract, but never fully release me. I'd fallen into a trap, somehow: a self-perpetuating cycle of pain and exhaustion and exasperated, strangling tears. Relief, when it did come, was brief. Almost as soon as I surfaced, another wave would come crashing down. A few days on land, only to be swept out to sea once more.

These were my wartime lungs. It was even worse than the East End. Not even Shorehaven helped. I had no choice but to make a new normal of it: attempting work, stumbling home early, barely making it upstairs. Neglecting details and snapping at subordinates, I frightened those who'd seen my collapse and unsettled newer hires. After years of shielding workmates, wielding my rare favor to deflect the boss's wrath, I was now a source of dread myself. I knew, on some level, this didn't bode well for my employment, but that seemed petty compared to what I was up against. Breathing was my job now, and a demanding labor it was: unpaid and fruitless, with no way to clock off. Unable to eat, retching from my coughs, my faith in death distorted, swinging wildly between terror and desire. I lost sight of the sacred. My patience and tenacity crumbled like sandstone. I simply couldn't cope.

After years of mostly managing at home, I now found myself in the hospital – four times in two months! No longer helped by house calls, pumps and powders, steams and adrenaline shots, I was a modern man; I needed *machines*. And ultimately, the hospital helped me get one of my own: an electric nebulizer the likes of which I'd only known pharmacists to own. Money was no object in my state, and those doctors were more than willing to suggest home remedies.

They'd clearly gotten sick of me.

Even Peter had – or so I assumed, in my groggy stupor. My condition was no easier for him. I bled him dry with my needs, adding shame to the dread and violence I'd been gripped by. In all my floundering, I'd pulled my lover down with me, ripping him away from work and friends, sleep and sanity. In a matter of months, he'd visibly aged. I was ruining him, just as I'd ruined my mother. And for what? I was alone in my struggle, no matter who was with me. Cut off from life yet wretchedly reliant on the living, clinging to the grounding rock of human touch, begging for relief that no one could give. After working so hard for my independence! Priding myself (however quietly) on being the main breadwinner. My lungs had no respect for my success. They stripped me of all pretense and worldliness, reducing me to a helpless child.

I'm sure there's a lesson in that, but I'm still too stubborn to learn it.

Yet another reason to live again, I suppose.

Peter went above and beyond, as much as he could – up at all hours, brewing coffee, meting out medication. Taking my hands and meeting my eyes, steering me back from the brink. There's a dark intimacy in being cared for, you know. I'm sure my illness bore some responsibility for the depth of our connection. I didn't just love him, after all. I *needed* him.

And I hated it.

I wanted an equal. I wanted fair play. I didn't want

the trinkets Peter bought me – charms and amulets said to heal and protect. I didn't want his Catholic prayer cards. It was crushing to see him so powerless, driven to superstition by my defects. Anguished at the hospital, again and again, as he played the role of indifferent flatmate. Fearing for my life, yet unable to hold me, sit with me, or even express his concern until we were home, hidden, cowering in sickly seclusion.

Still, Peter claimed disease was but a tollbooth, and the fee a meager one for what it granted him access to: my heart, my mind, my soul. My body.

But he could keep it.

I was tired of my body. Infuriated by it. Afraid of it. Bone-deep drained, all but hallucinating from the overwhelm: strong smells, roaring traffic, aches and emotions all rolling together as one. Nauseated by noise, trembling from remedies, stomach a burning knot of caffeine. I was skinny and clammy and, in every way, blue.

And I could hide none of it. Emasculated and ashamed, I broadcast my brokenness everywhere I went – earning precious little sympathy in the process. Friends diagnosed me as attention seeking; perhaps my growing fear of solitude wasn't a product of illness, but the motivating force behind it. I couldn't even argue. I'd lost my grip on logic, and I knew how needy I'd grown. However fancy my suit, I was a beggar. And of all things, you'd think a man would have *air*.

An older couple lived across the hall: the building's gruff, stocky repairman and his sweet, motherly wife. Roy and Rosie, I believe. Rosie had long brought us biscuits and leftovers, pitying us "sad bachelors" and hoping to find us "some good women" someday. Knowing my condition, she made a point to check on me when I was alone, and her instincts served her well. Twice she found me purple in bed, unable to reach my medicine, and I solemnly added her to the growing list of people who'd saved my life.

Still, I would've had almost anyone help before my parents. My poor parents, who'd done so much for me. They'd already been through this. They didn't need to know it was happening again.

My visits to Stamford Hill grew infrequent, but their consequences were heavy. Unable to control things, from my timing to my coughing to the functions of my senses, I'd become hungry. Starved for an anchor. Greedy for something yielding and earthy and subject to *rules*. Something I could *dominate*.

And I found that – or I thought I did – in my sister.

My most unfortunate sister.

I don't think she knew the root of our clashes. I'm not sure I did, for that matter. But I had my complaints, that's for sure. She'd dumbed herself down, wasting time in the mirror, erasing all traces of who she was meant to be. Her culture, her ancestry, her religion: all but obliterated. She hid her genius beneath the veneer of a common housewife. After how thoughtfully we'd been raised! After all the emphasis our parents put on intellect and ethics. It felt like she'd disowned us. Like she was ashamed. And I told her so.

Multiple times.

With no provocation, I'd trail her through the house, breathlessly ranting, utterly crazed. Mindlessly venting months of misery on the one target I half-saw as below me. After all, *I* had never traded in history. I stayed true to our origins, even in the face of prejudice and mockery. I even bore the stamp of an accent, yet I'd still advanced in life. Did she not remember the hardships of our grandparents, the poverty and the pogroms (as if I did)? Didn't she know what Jews now faced in Germany (like I understood)? Respecting our family was the least I could do, and it had cost me nothing.

Ada's rebuttals were unusually measured. She had plenty of munitions, but refrained from firing them. She could've called out my self-effacement, my questionable alliances, my eccentric home life. She could've weaponized the past, blaming her heresy on a youth full of offerings to my ungodly lungs. How often had she been held back, heeding my needs over her own? She could've called me a tyrant. But she didn't. She merely stated her duty as a mother: to set her children up for the best life that she could – and if that meant sacrificing to acculturate her son and daughter in their own native land, then so be it. No one cared about her ideas anyway; she was a simple woman. Integrity looked different from where she stood.

This objectivity was a bad sign. The lack of fire in her fight showed she'd lost all warmth for me. Her heart had grown cold. But, sleep-deprived and smothered, I wouldn't let it go: why would Ada even come for Shabbos, when she sent her children to church on Sunday? What sort of freaks was she raising that played with a dreidel under a Christmas tree? Distorting and diluting God's people into obscurity – just who was she trying to be?

My abuses met an abrupt end one afternoon upstairs, when Ada finally reached her breaking point. It seems I'd underestimated both her respect for me and her awareness: she knew about me and Peter. She'd seen us kissing in the garden. She'd heard our giggles through the wall. She'd known about us for years. And if I didn't stop ranting like a maniacal hypocrite, everyone else would too.

I held my tongue after that.

PRICK

AFTER HALF A dozen hospital stays, I knew the staff quite well. I particularly liked a nurse named Lucinda: a sweet, young Catholic who saw me not just at my worst, but also my best – polished and poised, on the Friday night bus to Stamford Hill. Before a chance encounter there, I usually took the train, but Lucy's company was pleasant enough to inspire the inconvenience. Off the clock, her dark humor came out, and she openly shared first-hand accounts of medical horror that put my lingering embarrassment to rest. Our rides together were never planned, but in time we came to expect one another. Despite doctrinal differences, she'd offer homemade treats for Shabbos, teasingly fussing over my health and appetite. Playful and pretty, with chocolate hair and coffee-cup eyes, I could almost see a life with her – far off in some parallel, utopian reality where life made sense.

As it was, I felt no man was worthy of her.

Likewise, she felt no doctor was any good for me. But she recommended one anyway: an alternative practitioner with a revolutionary approach. Her own sister was his secretary. They'd known him for years.

He worked wonders.

So I followed up on the suggestion. And that man changed *everything*. Not just my medication, either, not just my lung capacity – but the conversations I had, the way I thought, how I moved through life. My whole understanding of the world, of healing, of *being*: turned upside down and inside out.

Both for better and worse.

My protocol now involved exercise, stretches, and (ironically, given my past) yogic breathing, transplanted all the way from India. But it wouldn't be the first time one incarnation found its cures in another. We cherry-pick our challenges with a subtlety and savvy meant to confound our mortal minds; we're all geniuses, deep down, hell-bent on baffling ourselves. Practicing pranayama in Britain to ease the fallout from a previous life in colonial India is but one example of how dizzy our souls can get.

And my new doctor couldn't have said it better himself.

Like Peter, he harbored suspicions of supersensory ailments: past-life traumas, ancestral ties, telepathic stress triggering my asthma. But unlike Peter, he did not propose these things in jest; they were not to be taken with a grain of salt. This man was hardly a doctor at all, it seemed, but a shaman – a psychiatrist, an exorcist, a spiritualist. You can see how desperate I'd become. Under other circumstances, I'd have dismissed such flimflam without a second thought.

As things were, though, I happily embraced it.

The mystic East wasn't the only source of his notions, either. He was as open to anything as I was. Cutting-edge developments from America caught his eye, as did the nuances of physical therapy, ancient humoralism, and psychology. Vegetarianism was advocated – an easy option for me, as Peter hadn't eaten meat in years. But out of this whole eclectic array, one treatment stood above all others: a colorful take on somatic healing that quite literally brought me to my knees.

Traumatic events, it was posited, were stored in the body; repressed emotions expressed as disease. My bleak memories of the East End – the safe escape from war I was expected to feel grateful for – formed the basis of a habitual helplessness. No worries, though; those old anxieties could be pressed from my shoulders like juice. The whole experience of leaving Belgium, with all its bombs and babies, was beaten out of me with the skill and fury of a boxer. And the background buzz of my obvious *otherness*, the fears fueling my Zionist reveries, the strain of perpetual exposure: wrung out like water from a rag.

All I needed was to feel. *Experience* what I'd been through, *sensitize* myself to the intricacies of my body and mind – not numb them. No more throwing medication at my lungs like grenades in combat, no more making an enemy of my own anatomy. For once in my long fight for breath, my sensitivity was a strength. And at last, my efforts were paying off. Following each treatment, brutal though they were, I'd enjoy days, if not weeks, of relief.

Of course, it wasn't to last.

I don't want to explain what happened, but I'm not sure I have choice. Honesty is the antidote here. It was secrecy that ruined me, in the end. Pretending things were fine was precisely what made them *not*.

But it's confusing, even now. I was there on purpose, after all: stripped to my underwear, candid beyond measure. Letting that man twist and squeeze to his heart's content. I was asking for it.

The crumbling began with discussions of sex – for obvious reasons, the last thing I wanted to speak of. But there was trauma there, too: a second suffocation I'd willfully ignored. With love like Peter's – constant and soothing, celestial and safe – it felt like sacrilege to complain. But we lived on a diet of lies, and those lies ate at me in turn. Lies about work, lies about income. Should my parents see the scope of my success – should I buy a house or holiday abroad – there'd be no reason not to find me a bride. So Peter and I stayed small. Unmoving, unseen, hidden from the day like vermin. Perverts, addicts, criminals. A frightened pair of fugitives. At the end of the day, we burned like a candle under glass. The oxygen was sure to run out eventually. In truth, neither of us could breathe.

The doctor seemed sympathetic at first. So I loosened up. Told him more.

And that was the turning point. What was fresh began to sour, and that office became a stinking marsh. A swamp of slimy smiles and suggestive comments. A morass of manipulation.

Or so it seemed. Maybe it was just me.

Maybe the doctor's hands were meant to creep so low, maybe it was part of the treatment. Maybe my hips were holding tension. Maybe I needed this. Who was I to say? I certainly couldn't manage my body well – and this man, arguably, had saved my life.

Weeks went by in a thickening fog. I began to dread my appointments. My progress stalled. My enthusiasm waned. Yet for what? A vague discomfort? These procedures were *meant* to be uncomfortable! My agitation was a symptom of catharsis, for all I knew. An eruption of my own depraved thoughts. The sick projections of a sick mind.

My confusion soon turned to clarity, though. When the doctor's hands slipped deep below my waist one day, wrapped around the front, and took hold – I knew I wasn't imagining that.

I was timid, though. Worn down by doubt. I pulled back with a flurry of apologies, like I'd been the one to cross the line. Like I'd asked too much. Like I'd compromised the doctor's integrity myself.

But his professional confidence did not waver: "I thought you liked this."

I reminded him of my relationship, but he only laughed. *The homosexual is a promiscuous beast* – that's what he told me. A scarred psyche. A hungry wound. Incapable of monogamy, out only for pleasure. "Men like you don't *marry*."

I never went back.

And I never told anyone, either. How could I? After all the headway I'd made, it felt like self-sabotage. An overreaction to a minor incident I'd stupidly constructed myself. If I hadn't been so desperate, so eager, so *defective*, it never would have happened. Had I not run willingly to this man? Given over my body completely? I was a homosexual, after all – and what did I really know about that? Had I not, grotesquely, been aroused by his touch?

I grew cold with Peter; his own touches were only reminders. I ate less. I slept more. And how I dreaded going out! I took different busses, took the tube, haunted by thoughts of seeing Lucinda. And what if I were to see *him*? His office was nowhere near Mayfair, but stranger things had happened. London was large, yet I'd run into my father's colleagues unprepared. I'd seen my boss on weekends. I couldn't *truly* hide.

Asthma was almost welcome, for once. Back on my chest like it never left, it tied me to my bed, locking me in my room. But I knew it wasn't protecting me. It was punishing me. Serving up God's retribution in whopping doses.

My life was filth and sin and vanity, and I deserved no less.

My growing paranoia – that the doctor would report my confession, that arrest was imminent – would've felt fair were I the only one at risk. But I wasn't, and the danger I'd exposed Peter to gnawed at me. Made me jumpy and distracted. So mortified by my carelessness, I could hardly look him in the eye.

I didn't feel like a person anymore. No one's lover, no one's friend. Not an artist or authority. Not a man. Merely a creature. Unreachable, impotent – and unable to tell anyone why.

If I wanted to keep my secrets, though, I had to pull it together. Disgusted though I was with my body and its treacherous parts, I had to fix it. For work. For Peter. For little Annie. My niece and nephew knew a different me; they expected wrestling matches and tickling, smuggled candies, costumes, comedy shows. For them, I had to get my life in order.

I certainly wasn't doing it for myself.

So I studied. I read the books the doctor endorsed, though they all felt somehow sticky. I did each stretch he'd prescribed, despite my crawling skin. And all along, Peter was with me – researching reflexology, taking up yoga. Stalwart and dedicated, even as I balked at his advances.

It wasn't enough, though. I needed more. Professional guidance, state-of-the-art care. And perhaps, if I went to the source, things would be different. If I found the authors, the masterminds behind these techniques, maybe their medicine would be pure. Authentic. Uncorrupted. I just had to go where they were.

To Germany.

They were German doctors.

In my stifling cavern, I'd avoided the news. Cut off from friends, out of touch with relatives, scarcely able to work, politics had been the least of my concerns. Peter, however, suffered none of these setbacks. He'd kept right on meeting people, petitioning, reading his leftist magazines. He sheltered me, though, on account of my illness. My neurosis. My sublime sensitivity.

But his shield fell the moment I mentioned Bavaria.

I'd worked out the cost of a trip to Switzerland. A short stay in Davos – just a few weeks in a sanatorium – that was all I needed. After that, I'd be well enough to move about. Take a train to Munich. Meet these doctors in person and finally heal.

Peter said no, as did my parents. Even my sister took issue with my plans. Hadn't I been the one, not long ago, to bring up the plight of the German Jews? Had I lost my mind? I was to go nowhere near Germany – or anywhere on the Continent, for that matter.

I found this all bewildering. Were we not critical thinkers? Students of history, aware of society's tendency toward mass psychosis? Antisemitism was a catching virus, true, but so was paranoia. Fear had always made a profit. Who's to say those dark reports, those vague tales of persecution, weren't just hearsay? Gossip pushed to sell some papers? The news was hardly consistent. One day, Germany would be painted as nefarious; the next, an ally.

Peter, at least, should have understood this. It was *his* business, after all. Exaggeration simply greased the gears. But he would have none of it. The Germans were systematically targeting Jews, he said. And homosexuals. And the sickly, the disabled. The Germans were targeting *me*. These doctors I was so curious about – they wouldn't see me as diseased.

They'd see me *as disease.*

It hurt, being asked to heed such lunacy with my life on the line. Did no one want me healthy? I was finally holding the keys to my body, yet blocked from using them by the very people who claimed to love me. Those radical magazines Peter read, all that propaganda – it was making him hysterical. Daft, even. Violence against Jews was nothing new, but this? The way Peter made it sound, violence was being doled out from an itemized list, programmed and outlined by the state itself. Nothing like the spontaneous eruptions I'd grown up with. Nothing like the pogrom in Białystok, just weeks before my birth. And to wit: I'd still seen doctors in Białystok.

I must've sounded so selfish. Senseless and heartless and rash. But I was tired. Unendingly tired. So weary from drowning that politics was just another weight on my chest. In that soupy mire, I couldn't see anything clearly. I no longer knew what was real. It was probably for the best, how often I lost my voice.

Mere days after these arguments, anti-Jewish riots swept the streets of Germany. Staggering in size. Incomprehensibly brutal. Bloodcurdling. They knocked the wind from us all.

The Germans called it *Kristallnacht.*

TENSION

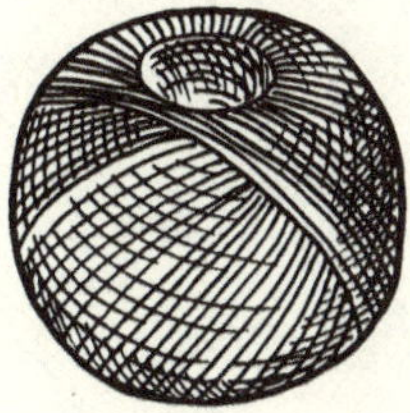

Reality hit hard when the Nazis entered Poland. Like a caterpillar in its cocoon, my whole cosmology underwent a rather horrifying change. Evil was real, after all – and organized. An efficient, fine-tuned machine. My final drops of optimism, my very lifeblood, dried up. Ashamed of how I'd behaved – ignoring such an obvious threat, blinded by my own misery – I slowly began to unravel. Withdrawing. Going silent.

You'd think, with my moralistic education, I could do better. *Be* better. But no.

Apparently it takes Peter's schooling to get it right. To grow up with injustice, to learn duplicity from your own parents: that's how you make good in the world. By sifting through the abuse, filtering out a keen eye, a commitment to honesty. Empathy. Awareness. To take on that task, to reform my psyche – that would be the least I could do. It's the only way to make up for things. Forge a life in which I don't just *take*.

Take, take, take. That's all I ever did.

Let me tell you, remembering this is hard. And not because of the bullet wound, now, not because of death; it's these feelings. So many feelings, like hot iron rods in the cold dark. But how do you describe heartache without a heart? Without up and down, without beginning and end. With no clear truth. No counterfeit. All I know now is pain. It's all I am.

There came a time when I realized everything: the atrocities taking place, the inevitability of war, the danger my loved ones faced abroad. And Britain changed its mind along with me. Until then, those in power had merely issued hand slaps – self-conscious *tsks* in the direction of a homicidal megalomaniac. They clearly hadn't been reading Peter's magazines.

That wasn't the only thing I realized, though – and that wasn't the only thing Peter had been right about. My health *was* tied up in this somehow. I *had* felt this coming, and I felt more coming still. The future rose like a tsunami: a great, solid wall of death, thick and broad. And the greater the tension in the air, the greater the trouble for my lungs. Maybe I'd never been separate. Maybe every flare-up I'd ever suffered had been linked to something else, somewhere else, unknown. Maybe my body did respond to war. Maybe I was a barometer.

I'm sure I seemed insane. My parents viewed me with pity: asthma and anxiety must've caught me in a maddening feedback loop. My sister rejected my every word. Only Peter entertained my rambling – albeit agnostically. But Peter wouldn't always be there. Pressed by family to be the hero his brother wasn't, and enraged by Germany's crimes, Peter was going to enlist. How he'd handle combat was up for debate, but his wish to join the common man could finally be granted in the army. That equalizing uniform, great eraser of class and creed, trumped all his pacifistic ideals.

Plus, it promised a break from me. War was an escape from the sickroom, and we both knew it – though neither of us had the nerve to say it aloud.

In the end, my battles were mine alone.

I knew I couldn't win. The assault of recognition was too heavy. Too strange. And amid my many epiphanies, one stood out as especially brutal: it was honesty that had won me my victories. Honesty, and nothing else. Airing my fears and traumas brought far more healing than exercise or massage. Getting the truth off my chest, more than anything, had made it feel lighter.

But true candor was impossible, and always had been.

So I studied in secret, poring over Peter's papers, scouring the underground for anything that might predict the fate of my lungs. And what I found was lethal: my family was in danger, and not just those in Poland. My aunts and uncles, my cousins, their children – the entire Jewish diaspora *needed to get out of Europe.* Our synagogue had rallied to help those in Germany – publishing, donating, working with Kindertransport – but there was no such outcry for Belgium or the Netherlands. Denmark. France. They were safe, I was told. No cause for alarm. *Calm down, Reuven. Focus on what's important.*

Overnight, I went from naïve apologist to

paranoid neurotic.

For the first time, Peter and I were on the exact same page. At last, I understood his angst and urgency. His loneliness. No one seemed to grasp the full monstrosity unfolding. No one was really *doing* anything.

So I took matters into my own hands. I made the wheezing slog across town to see my father's lawyer. I wanted immigration papers. I wanted to be prepared. But the logistics of it all, the convolution of bureaucracy – it wasn't something I was qualified for. I hadn't the fortitude to fight with words any more than with weapons. Foreign language had never been a strength of mine, and this was all Greek to me. With neither the skills nor the evidence to win legal favor, I caved at the lawyer's head-shaking and sighs.

I failed my relatives. Ultimately, most would be murdered – all because I was too stupid to understand juridical jargon.

Stupidity kills.

Not that it would've made much difference. My letters to the Continent fell on deaf ears. My extended family didn't take me any more seriously than my immediate one. I had no other way to fight, though. I couldn't join the service; I hardly even made it to the medical assessment. My health history, doctors' notes, and sorry state were enough to free me from *all* patriotic duties, in fact, not just military ones. I could carry on as usual, despite the world falling to pieces around me. Perhaps I could plant a garden – if I felt well enough, that is.

I didn't feel relieved. I felt guilty. Shame, frustration, and disappointment all competed for center stage. In the end, a generalized self-loathing took the spotlight.

Meanwhile, nearly everyone I knew headed off to training camps. Including Peter.

He was called to duty early in the war. I remember our last dance like it was . . . not quite yesterday. More like *now*. Like it's still happening. In a dance hall filled with soldiers, we sang to a brass band – "We'll Meet Again" – and believed every word. There are times, even now, when that song plays through this hollow, sung by the stars themselves: a disembodied echo of an ulcer that gnaws at me to this day. Eerie, howling, whispering, screaming, sobbing, laughing lyrics, chewing on whatever is left of me. Drenching me in tears. Showering me with kisses. Boiling me whole.

I still feel Peter in my arms. The starched wool of his jacket, the strength of his back. How handsome he looked in uniform, like those long-ago Tommies on parade. Most men at that dance had women on their arms, but we weren't the only anomalies. Old friends, we could have been – old friends, as so many assumed we were. And who would've stopped us from dancing then? Who, in the face of death? It's true that uncertainty makes people stiff; chaos can bring out the most controlling impulses. But at that moment, nothing could've kept me from Peter, and not one soul dared to prevent it. Perhaps we got some looks, perhaps some whispered words. But we were beyond caring. That night, our last night together, we couldn't have been more alone.

I just wanted to keep him. All I ever wanted was to keep him, just like that, forever. The smell of him, his glistening eyes, his caramel laugh. It's a chasm now, where he was. A maddening sensation. Fingers I no longer have, running through open air. Arms long gone, holding nothing.

He left me with a jasper ring and these final words: "Do right by yourself, Reuven."

Oh, Peter. My Peter.

What torture to feel him now, knowing I shouldn't have him! Taunted by that song. Pecked at. Ground down by its mechanical teeth. They played it on the radio relentlessly. Throbbing, aching, longing.

Would I be able to escape it, if I moved on? If I went back to face what I deserved, in a new body, a new life? Or would I still be haunted, confounded by cruel, teasing clues – unable to weave a coherent picture?

Perhaps that song would still make my stomach sink. Or perhaps it would only be a song.

On the last day of 1939, a gunshot rang out in my kitchen. It was early morning, bleak and chilly, and I'd been standing at the sink. The sound was earsplitting, shattering the still of my whole building. As I stumbled through the flat, looking for the source, three separate neighbors came to see what had happened. I had no explanation for them. Nothing was amiss at all.

It must've been the ghost.

FRAY

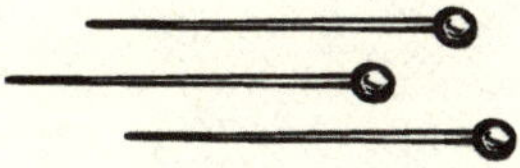

SEVERAL BOMBS FELL before the Germans began dropping them. The first involved my job: we were downsizing. Thanks to fabric rationing, pattern making took precedent, and due to my experience (and so many workmates abroad), I was promoted to management – hardly a welcome advancement given my health. Bomb number two brought similar side effects: it seemed the entire medical system collapsed – at least from where I stood. The physicians and nurses I'd come to rely on took their services to the front, leaving me scrambling for care when I needed it most. Arguing with strangers on the severity of my condition. Crippled in a gas mask yet unable to secure an invalid respirator, I couldn't convince new doctors it wasn't all in my head.

No one could vouch for me. Everyone was leaving.

Yet I endured.

Lonely and bored and fearful and disgusted with myself, I passed my time writing letters, playing piano, staring at the wall. My sister went to work in a factory. Her husband trained as a fighter pilot. My mother organized gardening efforts. My father raised money for refugees, assisting families who'd taken in Jewish children from Germany. I slept odd hours and coughed up blood.

Life was making a mockery of me.

Propaganda applauded women on the home front, posters dripping down city walls, littering the tube, paving the streets: grow food, earn your keep, support your men abroad. And yet *I* was the audience. *Me.* Helping my mother can vegetables. Mending and sewing and knitting. Waiting for my sweetheart to come home.

I was no man. I couldn't fight. I couldn't kill the enemy – I couldn't even help their victims.

Belgium fell to the Germans, as did Holland, just as I'd predicted. But no one commended my foresight. I renewed my campaign of letters, trying to connect not only with relatives, but with anyone I knew by name. How could I face myself, refugee that I was, if I couldn't share my sanctuary? I visited a different lawyer. I'd put people up in my own flat if I had to. But still, no one felt the desperation I did. They hadn't watched that baby vanish in war's waters. They didn't know what it was like to drown, nor could they see the incoming wave. Or if they did, they were resigned to it.

Slip.

Gone.

The third bomb fell early that summer: Peter was dead.

He'd been dead for weeks before I knew, killed near Brittany sometime in June. But no one could tell me exactly how or where, and, of course, I received no official notification. No date or time or cause of death. Nothing to fill in the details but the spiked bludgeon of imagination. I had visions of explosions, fire and blood: nightmares of my lover entombed in a ship, drowned in black water and oil. Another meal for war's hungry seas, bound to me in mutual suffocation. Helpless as he choked, after all he'd done for me. Smothered in darkness, after being my beacon. Calling to me. Across space and time, crying out his fate.

But no reports of such a tragedy came, however vivid and insistent my dreams – and no illuminating word could reach me. No documents tied Peter back to me. No legal bond. Fifteen years of dedication notwithstanding, I was still no one's spouse.

My first clue had been the lack of letters. Until mid-June, Peter wrote ceaselessly – mostly about training, friends, the news. But also love. At least a drop of love, always, if not a whole surge. It was hard to believe, though, as he risked his life and I did nothing. Trapped in the inanity of fabric scraps and gossip, I didn't deserve the love he sent.

But I wouldn't have to worry about that anymore. He was dead.

Along with everything else.

I went to the Barnetts when I caught word, unsettled by a series of ominous, unexpected condolences. I needed to know if the rumors were true. I needed it straight from those with the telegram. I bought a bouquet and suffered the itchy-eyed bus ride to Kensington. I'm not sure what I expected. I suppose I wished to know where he was buried. I wished, at least, to properly mourn.

One look at his mother and sister confirmed the worst, but beyond that I got no closure from my half-mad visit. In fact, in the thickening smog of censorship, I doubted they knew much more than I did. But they blamed me, nonetheless. Blamed me as I teetered there, hollow and winded on their front porch – for the madness of nations, for the war itself. For Peter's death. They blamed my family, my relatives, my ancestors. And then they claimed, with a soul-socking conviction, that the least of Peter's concerns had been the self-pitying, so-called "plight" of the Jewish race. He'd wanted no more to do with *my kind* than they did. And that included me.

I certainly wasn't allowed in.

They took the flowers, though.

So I started crying. Almost daily, crying: on the bus, on the street, in alleyways. In the toilet at work. In my flat, with that ridiculous ghost rattling the dishes – too ravaged and delirious to be scared. Crying until my ribs ached. Crying until I threw up. Choked by my tears yet unable to stop them, I was alone in a whirl of pain and confusion as the world succumbed to chaos.

I could hardly comprehend my life now. What was I even mourning? What had I really lost? No one could tell me. I had no one to grieve with. No body, no funeral, no explanation or acknowledgment. No way to sit shiva; there was simply no precedent.

I said the Kaddish and lit a candle, but a breeze blew it out, and my mind went with it. Peter's death felt groundless. Impossible. Imaginary. Like he'd never existed. We were merely flatmates to many. Friends, at most. It surely wasn't holy devotion. Not a *calling*, sacred and divine. Not a healing balm, medicine for the masses, curative and communal. Not a steady, rhythmic, magical, transformative passion. Not love like the moon.

Only my father seemed to grasp how I felt. Thanks to the very same scrutiny that had pushed me away, I now shared a strange closeness with him. He'd studied me well, after all; he knew what had died. But while his sympathy was clear, the topic was just too taboo. We couldn't truly talk about it.

It was like it never happened.

And hadn't I gone crazy in other ways? What in my mind could I even trust anymore?

Maybe Peter's family was right. Maybe our whole affair had been one-sided. A decade-plus delusion. He had to have been disgusted with me, after all – a crippled Jew, addicted to sexual perversion. An incoherent, mucus-spewing monster. Not even my workmates wanted me around; they eyed me like a time bomb. Like a dead man walking. Childishly resorting to illness to meet my needs. Willing to die for attention. I knew I wasn't loved. I wasn't even liked. There's no way a man of Peter's caliber would have had me. *Who would ever have me?*

There came a moment, in that hallucinogenic stupor, when I latched onto Peter's family. Soul like an octopus, I suckered to them, swearing allegiance, handing myself over in the next life before even finishing the one I still lived. In that broken, disoriented world – with private secrets and state-sanctioned lying – that family seemed so *certain*. While I wallowed in nuance and doubt, the madness of intuition and the psychosis of war, they found *fact*.

Never mind that intuition is all you have in war; I was in no position to chase autonomy. I couldn't even breathe. My brain had gone limp, suggestible as a nation under attack. Lost in propaganda, I had nothing left but feeling. Fear. Anger. Anguish. And above all, shame. Shame at my weakness. At my neediness, my filth. Shame at the unknowable atrocities I was a party to in my ignorance. My helplessness. My selfishness.

Idealism was dead, and I had no idea how to function without it. Life rubbed me like sandpaper, the news like a saw blade. Peter's family was the one place where words made sense. The Barnetts, and only the Barnetts, said aloud what I was thinking. In them I found a match. I hooked on like a parasite.

I took a train to Seaford one weekend. Then a cab to Shorehaven. I knew the back bedroom window didn't latch. I climbed through it like a criminal, driven to depravity by despair.

There had been fighting in the sky, both to the east and the west. There was no telling when the Germans might make landfall. Deranged though I'd become, I had no plans to calm down – to self-soothe with Zionist daydreams like my parents. Palestine wasn't an option to me anymore. We'd already been pushed from our country by violence once – arguably twice – and I had no interest in repeating history. London was my home now, and I would not be branded with a star and made an outsider in my own city. It was time to stop searching for belonging and start *demanding* it.

There was a gun at Shorehaven. An antique pistol. I knew it still worked: Peter's father was known to take it fox hunting – issuing some silly, ceremonial shot to commence the chase. Peter and I had taken it out ourselves once, hoping to shoot some ducks. We'd missed every one.

I took the gun and its bullets from a glass case in the front room. I wasn't sure what protection it could offer, especially against a whole army. I wasn't even sure I had it in me to kill. But I was sick of my cowardice. Disgusted by my lack of action. Appalled that Peter's sacrifice might be for nothing. Again and again, my attempts to affect things had been thwarted. I felt personally under siege.

But not much could stop a bullet.

CUT

THE BLITZ BEGAN in September.

There's a lot of talk in wartime of being strong. Of putting on a smile. Keeping a stiff upper lip. But it's all rubbish. The only people unbroken by war are sociopaths doomed to abuse others, passing their pain down through their descendants until it's an unrecognizable, unsolvable tumor.

Not that crumbling gives you a pass. None of my sobbing helped anyone.

The Luftwaffe targeted the East End first, and I felt that blow viscerally. How I'd hated the East End! Yet did it deserve those air raids? Did I ever wish such brutality on my old neighbors? Jews, many of them: stranded under a falling sky. After I'd so railed against my sister for turning her back on our people, here I sat doing nothing.

I began to feel I had no right to call myself Jewish at all. No right to call myself anything.

When the bombs began to rain over the West End, I welcomed it. It's what I deserved. Yet that thought only deepened the guilt. I wasn't the only one suffering. Businesses shuttered and shut down. Windows were boarded. The whole city dragged itself underground, cowering every sunset, each time those hellhound sirens issued their howl.

A few years before, there'd been a fire: an elaborate glass structure – equal parts greenhouse, concert hall, and museum – had burned to the ground. I'd only seen it a few times, but I always liked it. I figured it'd be there, should I chose to return. I trusted its presence. Its sudden absence was palpable.

This was infinitely worse.

Places I'd leaned on, believed in, taken for granted as integral parts of a natural landscape, disappeared over night. Hollow husks, serrated claws, smoking peaks of rock and ash – this was the world now. Primordial. Disorienting. Reforged every day in new, nightmarish ways. I failed to help search the debris; the dust was unbearable. I failed to help clear the roads; I tripped on a human arm.

It was November 16, in the wee hours, when reality tumbled down. After so much teetering, weakening, staggering like a drunkard, one dreary night it finally collapsed. I'd taken shelter, as usual, in the basement of a store up the street. We had cots and sleeping mats, a stash of biscuits; it certainly could've been worse. But there was never any air, and my lungs were acting up that evening. Demanding more than I was prepared to give. People were still filing in, though – the doors were still open. So I left alone to get my medicine, past strangers heading the other way, hauling blankets and teacups and hot water bottles, shooting nervous glances at the sky.

I'd planned to come right back, but I hardly

made it to my flat. Wheezing along with the sirens, climbing the stairs did me in. I spent that night in bed, raw and exposed, enduring what felt like the worst asthma attack of my life.

Though who could really say? I was also being bombed.

The sky erupted out the window: a collage of flashes, jagged and erratic. Some distant, some deafeningly close. Rattling dishes, shaking the building loose at its seams – like a train was crashing through. And there I struggled, strangled, fighting for every worthless breath in a darkness broken only by fire. Unsure if my nebulizer had power. Unable to dig up the black balloon. I didn't even have a glass of water.

I'd never felt so alone. Marooned, floating, lost in space. This was an alien planet, a nightmarish landscape of nauseating, rust-flavored noise: planes growling with an ocean's rage, unleashing a relentless, screaming bombardment – whistling and hammering, the whole earth shuddering. Caving in. And I couldn't breathe. I couldn't breathe. Drowned and discarded, my house collapsing, the streets on fire and thick with smoke. Dying, right then and there. Unsure just what would finish me off, but wedded to death. Swallowed by its certainty, merged with it. I no longer recalled a before, no longer hoped for an after. Time had closed its mouth on me. I waited only to be digested. Wanting to scream – *trying* to scream – but unable even to whisper.

I was the only soul alive that night. As good as dead.

I don't remember it ending. I lost consciousness at some point, waking the next day to a smoldering street: a neighboring storefront vomiting rubble, nearby buildings no better off.

Likewise, I would never be the same.

I spent most nights with my parents after that, only going to Mayfair to work. Not that I *worked.* I panicked: flinching at laughter, jumping when doors slammed, losing my temper over car horns and bicycle bells, overwhelmed by sound and flavor. I simply couldn't function. I bore half the responsibility for the business, but could hardly remember what the business even was. I gave my workmates countless reasons to doubt my fitness, yet I couldn't care less.

And neither could they, apparently.

I wasn't heartened by their forgiveness. I took no comfort in their patience with me. If anything, it made me feel disposable. Like my work didn't matter at all. Did I offer so little that my failings affected *nothing*? If negligence and truancy couldn't get me fired, why had I been hired to begin with? I certainly hadn't come by my status honestly; I knew I'd stolen it. My rank was due to nothing but the absence of others. Others more qualified, others more reliable. Others now laying their lives down to protect people like me. Superfluous, incompetent *me.*

And to think, I'd been so frightened of losing my job! My health hadn't threatened things, after all. Nothing did. I was irrelevant. A pity case, a joke. Feeble and gutless at work, at home, in a doctor's office. My body had escaped the bombs, but still, I took a direct hit. No corner of my psyche was spared. My history, my sense of self, all that I found meaningful: too fragile to withstand the blast. Everything crumbled.

Though Stamford Hill didn't feel much safer, it was clear I couldn't live on my own anymore. It was only a matter of time before I moved back. Useless, fanatical Reuven, home again, with all his coughing and gasping and needs. Needs on top of needs on top of needs.

For the time being, though, I still had my flat. Mine and Peter's, once upon a time. And I'd go there almost daily – mostly just to wail at the walls.

I was mad. Fully mad. Ranting at the air, pulling at my hair. Clattering the dishes back at Ferdinand, even breaking one myself. Begging the specter for a sign, pleading for ghostly memories. Surely, Ferdie had also fallen for Peter; who wouldn't fall for Peter? Soulful, pure, and giving – Peter alone had held me together. Peter alone contained my parts. I was fractured now: split into bits, known only in snippets, like newspaper headlines without elaboration. No one knew what I thought or felt. No one knew my spirit, the wilderness of my suffering, the fanaticism of my love. No one knew me.

Hours were spent rereading his letters, weeping over old photos – all left pooling like blood on the floor, loosing my secrets in the end. Peter's journals disclosed tenderness, bitterness, staggering hope; I scattered them about in daze. One by one, I collected our objects, odd little items I'd take back to Stamford Hill: souvenirs to remind me of us. I cut Peter's clothes into handkerchiefs, hacking and wheezing into his absence with every attack.

Which was nightly, now. Every time I heard the air raid sirens.

No sound so suited the end of the world; nothing made the walls fold quite like it. As if asthma wasn't frightening enough, my fits now sprung from fear's belly itself. A fear made worse by news from the Continent, coming in ever-darker waves: reports of business closures, radio confiscations, increasing brutality. Exactly what I'd vainly predicted.

While my father read his brothers' letters aloud, I read mine in horrified silence. They came mostly from one cousin – a woman in Amsterdam, an old playmate from Antwerp. A shopkeeper, now. A mother. And the sole sympathetic ear to my early "paranoia."

But her writing stopped eventually, just like Peter's.

Unlike Peter, however, I knew every detail of her death: an accident so poorly prevented, you'd think it was on purpose. Prearranged spontaneity. A planned random tragedy. She'd been cornered in an alley one night, ringed by Germans and German shepherds.

Killed by dogs.

Chewed like food. Mauled to death.

Dogs.

My dreams of Peter came back with a vengeance. Burns on his arms. Oil spilling through portholes. And singing – distant, obscene, terrifying singing – as that mighty ship sank under. "Roll Out the Barrel," of all things. I found myself humming it. I made myself sick with it.

My brain was being damaged from lack of oxygen.

In an airless void, my days began to slow. Each passing hour stretched out long, feverish and phantasmal. And every night: a thunderous abyss. Time marched forward no longer, but retracted like a snail in a shell. Curling up. It became a whirlpool, dragging me down. I was sinking.

Imagine, if you will, that life is a ball. Each and every one of us: a rubber ball, thrown into the world at birth by a careless hand. Perhaps we'll hit something, bounce back. Perhaps we'll crash wildly between unseen obstacles. Or perhaps we'll remain aloft, flying smooth and free and straight until, at last, gravity takes us down. We'll bounce up once, then down again. Then up. Then down. Each time we rise, it's less than before – until we're only rolling. And finally, we stop.

That had been my life: high and smooth and free. But now I was bouncing. Tea with my parents – a tunnel of fog – a stroll with my sister – a serpentine cave – a board game with Annie – immobilizing pain.

The war looked endless and unwinnable, and I couldn't fight. Couldn't save my relatives. Couldn't care for myself or manage a job. My city was burning, and I couldn't put out the fire. Thousands were dying, yet there I sat: padded with pillows, waited on hand and foot, drawing dresses.

I was a spoiled, self-absorbed, delusional beast.

Wanted by no one, yet terrified of being alone. Nothing but a waste of time.

I wasn't entirely powerless, though. I had one last option.

On the last day of 1940, a gunshot rang out in my kitchen. It was early morning, bleak and chilly, and I'd been standing at the sink. The sound was earsplitting, shattering the still of my whole building. As I tumbled over and hit the floor, three separate neighbors came to see what had happened.

I had no explanation for them.

I was dead.

SCRAPS

I VIVIDLY RECALL my last moments: heart racing, shaking, scratching out a short note. Handling the gun like bloody meat, loading it over the sink. Fumbling as I did so, but managing. Fingers far away, at the end of a long, dark corridor. Europe, London, the room around me – already lost, already gone. The whole universe was just my hands, grey and distant and trembling.

And then I did it.

For half a minute I lay paralyzed on the floor, freezing, nauseous, lopsided where my skull once was. Whatever told my lungs to breathe was dripping down the wall, but one eye still functioned. Mindless and numb, I gaped at my innards – dizzying hues of red and peach, a neon bed of roses spinning farther and farther away – as I waited out my final suffocation.

Slip.

Gone.

Just a moment in time. Just one little moment.

I could've been doing anything else. But I was doing that.

My third death didn't bring the divinity I'd once known. Blissful, cleansing rivers of light don't bend to human will. Some things just can't be forced.

I was water for a while. I flowed the creeks and rivers near my old shtetl – now lost to the earth, hardly a sign left of ever existing. I lazed down the Supraśl, though I didn't know its name. Didn't know what I was or what it was or where or who or why. I was stripped, completely. Vacuous. A porous vessel, able only to receive: sticks and stones and animal scat. Human bodies. Incapable of judging or defining any of it. Differentiating at all – or even knowing that I could – simply sowed nightmares of mammoth proportion. Dissolution on a cosmic scale.

It was best just to surrender.

There's a branch of Kabbalistic thought that claims murderers come back this way. Reborn to flow, like the blood they once spilled. I must've been aware of it. I must've found it fitting.

For I was, indeed, a murderer.

Blinded by shame, deafened by a world screaming in pain, I'd taken the life of a Jew myself. I'd slaughtered the invalid. I'd shot the homosexual with my own bullet. And with that life, as with every life, went memories. History, stories, flavors and recipes, songs and cities and secrets. Wisdom and meaning, rich and vibrant: splattered on a kitchen wall. Never to be shared. Lost forever.

I was no better than the Nazis.

I evaporated and fell, rain over the Warsaw ghetto. Collected in a cup by a thirsty child. Carried from his belly to his veins, and pumped through his racing heart as he was thrust onto a stinking, serried train and lugged off to his death. He also had asthma, that poor little boy. He died on arrival at Treblinka. Kicked like a stray. Smothered in the dust while the rest of his family was gassed. Another "little bird," flown away.

I left him through a frothy spittle. Dried on his face. Licked at by flies.

I rained down again over the ocean, and there I crashed and swirled and self-digested until every last grasp at identity was beaten from me. Until I was truly nothing. Impeccably dead.

And then I washed up at Cuckmere Haven, just below the Seven Sisters. And I knew where I was. And I began to remember. I began, again, to *be*.

And here I am.

I know that it was fated, the life I chose, start to finish. But you get a lot of time to think in this place, and what's left of the mind does wander. I can't help but wonder what else could have been. Most imagined futures look bleak: a ruined career, a pathetic life at my parents' house. Devouring them with my misery. Strangled, in the end, by my own body. Drowned in pea soup.

But maybe I could've helped myself. Moved to the country. Found fresh air and a fresh start. Given my family a bucolic escape. I was a good tailor, after all; I could've found work almost anywhere.

I could've organized with my mother and sister. Embraced the feminine role I'd been thrust into. Taken my savings and bought a vacant lot, creating a garden for the whole community. At the very least, I could've sat with my parents through their unspeakable losses, comforting them as their brothers and sisters disappeared. Bearing witness. Holding them. Helping them. Being their *son.*

I could've found purpose. Purpose would've done me a world of good.

But none of that happened. It took less than one second to slam that door.

No more family. No more fabric. No more sketches and stitches or buttons and lace. No more bad days, no more good days. No more asthma. No more sea breeze. No more Shabbos candles, no more Seder plates. No more coffee. No more parties. No more delicious music. No more loose ties or glasses or mispronunciations. No more alley cats. No more air raids. No more jangling, smoky, bustling London.

No more possibility.

No more Reuven.

Slip.

Gone.

And what a tragic error of judgment. Hoping to spare my parents a burden, I'd only worsened their load – trading incidental inconvenience for a multigenerational ache. I left a body unfit for Taharah or proper burial. I left a father scraping his child's brains from kitchen cabinetry, haunted by thoughts of a headless son's resurrection. I received no eulogies. No public grief. I merely descended, liquid through the cracks, into the collective consciousness of blood. An unspoken pain. An inherited disease.

My death: repressed.

My life with Peter: denied.

All my many weaknesses: skillfully and violently cut out of time.

I became the skeleton Ada pushed aside when she hung her coats and dresses. The reason my parents moved from Stamford Hill, haunted by the fact that I never said good-bye. And I was the primal wound, the infected core, the shattered foundation of sweet little Annie's entire life.

Annie, who loved me above everyone. Annie, whom I'd failed to consider at all. Only ten years old when her hero, friend, and loyal confidant put a bullet through his own head. Ten years old, and the person she most adored abandoned her for death.

She was a smart girl. She knew what that meant. She wasn't enough for me.

And she wasn't allowed to talk about me.

Like the rest of my family, she trudged on, through the incomprehensible shock of the Shoah, into the pillowy caress of the '50s. But her heart remained hard. I'd broken her trust even more than the war, and no one could mend it. Not the husband she'd have, not the children she'd raise. I'd left her with a secret yet shareable loss. A contagious fear. A genetic mutation her descendants still carry: pathological unworthiness, ancient and festering, origins long since forgotten. My gift to my family – my legacy – has boiled down to an unknowable wound.

And unless I'm untangled from its roots, there may never be a cure. My memory, somehow, must be unearthed and exposed. Wounds need to breathe. What is life without air, anyway?

So I'm doing what I can. I'm telling my story. I'm admitting my crimes. It's the least I can do before moving on, succumbing once more to the amnesia of life. I know, from a certain point of view, that the pains I caused were needed: preordained scenes in a scripted play, enabling my loved ones to grow. But suffering only begets suffering; no injury ever heals another. There must be more than this cyclical misery.

To be entirely honest, this wasn't the first time I took my own life. I did it in India, as well. Having realized too late the extent of my errors, all my misguided writing and speaking and social climbing, big game hunting with British imperialists – I strung up a rope and hung myself. Asphyxiating then, and for decades thereafter.

The sad truth is once you've taken that plunge, the drop seems far less frightening. Self-destruction can be an awfully hard habit to break. One has to retrace the needle pricks to unthread that stitch – but actually stay with the pain. *Feel* it. Get angry if need be, rant and rave at the injustice of living. There's nothing sacred in pretending you're well. Lord knows I could've done more raging.

Instead I ran away. Escaped into duality, those polar extremes I knew so well: right and wrong, pious and debauched, healthy and desperately sick. But nothing is black and white.

Even suffering can be a blessing.

Immigration broadened my mind, war underscored my values, sexuality curbed my dogma. Even illness was a blessing, sinister though it seemed. Without it, I'd have been smothered by convention. Muzzled by marriage. I'd have never met Peter. Never known his grace or grit or astonishing humanity. It was sickness that pierced the veil, after all, revealing the ecstasy of release. It was pain, perhaps more than anything, that revealed God's love.

There's no way around it. The only way out is through. It won't be easy, adjusting to a new body, having left the old in such a fashion. My father's resurrection fears weren't entirely unfounded; I'm sure I've saddled myself with simply *exquisite* migraines. But I'll make use of discomfort, even when I can't recall its cause. Learn to fly, even in life. Spread my wings, release control, and let the winds have me. Then God can have me, too.

This time will be different.

I'll soon forget what I've shared here, but it'll remain all the same. What's done is done, and there's nowhere to start but where I left off. I'll face madness first, as Peter did. Make a home among the wolves. Turn inside out from doubt and lies. Cave in from the abuse, but dig myself out – excavating inner gems. Pressed diamonds of clarity and compassion, strength and discernment. Direction. Purpose. Just like Peter.

And perhaps, after that, I'll be worthy of him once more. Worthy of love: the most effective medicine I know.

But now I should go. I've taken far too much of your time. I didn't mean to, believe me. I lived such a little life; I had no idea I had so much to say about it.

I'm done now, though.

You can go. I know you've got things to do.

I do, too.

ABOUT THE AUTHOR

Writer, mystic, and hobby surrealist, H.B. Cavalier uses fiction to untangle psychic knots, explore collective karma, and heal past lives. *Unthreaded* is her second book, following the darkly comedic magical realism novel *Farewell, Everything*, which was published under the pen name Véva Perala. When she's not channeling war ghosts, she enjoys traveling, gardening, and creating art with her small family.

ALSO AVAILABLE FROM NOWHERE PRESS

●○

FAREWELL, EVERYTHING

In a world waking from a dark age, a young musician finds himself thousands of miles from home, covered in bruises, and falling in love.

And it's only downhill from there.

Chronically clueless and incurably naïve, runaway street performer Osha Oloreben has known his share of hard knocks – but none like those he's dealt in the city of Valena. Dragged into war and battered by disease, Osha unwittingly trades his life for a fever dream of half-truths and hidden realms. Helped and hindered by a cast of mystics, rebels, and ghosts, he struggles to reclaim his body, his identity, and reality itself – before it's too late.

With humor and horror in equal measure, *Farewell, Everything* delves into the dissolution of a transforming mind. Stumbling through the stages of grief – denial, anger, bargaining, depression, and acceptance – our unlikely hero braves the surreal landscapes of love, loss, and death, from which no one emerges unchanged.

○●

Farewell, Everything (2019) by Véva Perala is available in paperback and ebook. Visit **nowherepress.com** or **farewelleverything.com** to learn more.